Renovating Hell
LETTERS OF CONTENTION

J . E . S E R R A N O

 www.trafford.com

North America & international
toll-free: 844-688-6899 (USA & Canada)
fax: 812 355 4082

Steve Berger
Cover Designer

ACKNOWLEDGMENTS

Dedicated to my mother, whose strength and wisdom kept me on the straight and narrow when the road to temptation was wide and inviting.

Martin Duffy—friend, brother from another, and patron—who helped make my books possible.

Steve Berger, whose beautiful artwork depicted my vision.

My brother Hector Serrano, a.k.a. DJ Hecky Hottraxx, for your input.

Last but never least, my lady Denee, whose patience, love, and strength helped me navigate the chaos that is life.

Finally, to the readers, who took their most valuable time to read the book. I hope you enjoyed reading as much as I did writing. May the gates of Perdition be closed to you.

Thank you.

CONTENTS

PROLOGUE

From the depths of infinity, the Lord called forth his firstborn to converse—a conversation that would again reshape the universe. They observed nebula clouds, the birthplace of stars that exploded with brilliance as into life. The Creator addressed his first creation.

"I didn't and don't mind that you have a different opinion than me. When you wanted to get your own place, did I stop you?" the Creator of all inquired playfully.

Lucifer looked sideways at the Creator. "Well, it's not like you threw me a farewell party if I remember correctly," he said mockingly.

The Creator looked lovingly at his creation. "You know the others wouldn't have understood. They would have regarded it as a form of favoritism," the Creator pointed out.

Lucifer seemed to pout. "Do you mean to say I'm not your favorite?"

The Alpha smiled warmly. "Be that as it may, it just so happened to be the perfect justification and timing for your exit and do as you wished," the Alpha said pointedly.

Lucifer shook his head. "Expulsion," Lucifer corrected. "Saying exit implies that I left of my own volition."

"Tomatoes, potatoes, same difference," the Alpha dismissed. Lucifer shook his head in disbelief. "I just think," the Alpha continued, "with all that's going on and the direction these mortals are taking, it seems prudent to me that we are prepared for a massive population surge into Hell."

Going on as if the previous conversation had reached a conclusion, the exile bowed his head. "Thy will be done, but I don't think you've considered the amount of resistance this is going to cause."

The Alpha smiled at his son. "I suppose that is possible," the Alpha quipped.

The exile returned the smile. "No disrespect intended."

The Alpha nodded. "None taken. We are in agreement then?" the Creator asked.

The exile shook his head. "When have we ever been in agreement? That said, I will make efforts to see your will be done."

The Alpha glowed warmly. "You're such a good son."

The exile blushed. "Don't tell anyone," he whispered as he disappeared in a cloud of smoke.

The Alpha smiled. "Your secret is safe with me," he whispered back, knowing full well the exile heard.

CHAPTER

1

Lucifer returned to Hell, perturbed at the Creator's seemingly callous dismissal and admission that a substantial amount of mortals were not only seeing their demise but their apparent damnation as well. Lucifer sat behind his ornate huge ebony desk, grabbed a quill, and composed what he knew to be the first of many letters. Ibliss, Lucifer's personal assistant, stuck his head into his master's chambers. Seeing him bent over the table scribbling, Ibliss slowly left the chambers, somewhat concerned as the master of Hell rarely sat to such menial tasks.

A Letter of Holding and Intent

A demonic palace messenger was summoned and handed a missive and seal of transport that allowed him unfettered access through all the realms of Hell and woe to the foolish demon that tried to impede the royal messenger. Approaching the temple of traitors, the messenger waited to be noticed. One did not enter the ninth circle unattended as Glabrezu tended to Satan, who was chained in the frozen lake of Cocytus. Chained though he might be, his evil intent permeated the ninth circle and would lash out at any and all visitors. After a brief period, Glabrezu received the missive and delivered it to Abbadon.

From: The Desk of Lucifer, Firstborn, Angel of Light
To: Abbadon, King of Locusts, Ninth Circle
Cc: Glabrezu, Regent
Bcc: Eight remaining circles and their respective kings

This is a notification to all denizens of Hell. Let it be known that Hell will be undergoing a massive renovation, reconstruction, and modernization of all environs, including but not limited to the infernal treasury. Any and all inconveniences will be tolerated and suffered as appropriate for a denizen of Hell. All complaints will be addressed in an upcoming communiqué. Your fullest cooperation is expected. Any and all resistance or obstruction will be dealt with severely. Some will inevitably suffer and be displaced. (Welcome to Hell.) Those who suffer disproportionately shall be considered for reprobation although unlikely to garner any real satisfaction. (Again, Hell).

May your suffering be eternally exquisite.

Yours spitefully,
Lucifer
Angel of Light

   Abbadon paced in his chambers, clicking his talons. Upset by the letter sent by the Dark Palace, the angel of the bottomless pit wondered what Lucifer was thinking to change what took thousands of years to build! Hell was forged by the Angels, Perdition, Lucifer, and Samgina when they were cast from Heaven and carved by Mulciber, the great architect. Joy was not a feeling that was encouraged in Hell, that is, unless misery was to follow. As Abbadon understood the letter, Lucifer was implying that Hell was going to get very busy soon, and that meant the delightful sound of wicked and the occasional misplaced good soul being tortured for their sins, something that always gave Abbadon that feeling that was akin to joy. With anticipation for the uproar that was surely to follow such a seeming unprecedented event. *At least it won't be boring,* he mused.

Abbadon glanced around his chambers that held items of power and destiny—ravaging locusts and the keys to the bottomless pit, which would release the fury of Hell upon the mortal world. He heard the wailing of Satan trapped in the frozen lake of Cocytus. Satan, the aspect of Lucifer that embodied his wrath-filled and traitorous nature, was howling, sensing an opportunity to wreak havoc. Abbadon smiled an evil grin and called for Glabrezu, his vicegerent, who, knowing his master's mind, snatched up a quill. When Abbadon began dictating, Glabrezu began writing.

> From: Abbadon, King of Locusts, Angel of Pit
> To: The royal houses, staff, cadre, residents, and condemned of Hell
>
> It came to pass that at the end of the twentieth century, mankind had peered into the depths of the cosmos, split the atom, and gazed into the subatomic. He has also probed into the darkest pit of a black hole but still does not know all the workings of his own nature. Nor has he learned to live in harmony with his environment and, in his rush to control everything, never learned to control his baser instincts. So for his unending wars and total lack of regard for his fellow beings or the planet in which he resides, we have been so ordered by *the Chairman* and *the Supervisor* that Hell will be undergoing mass renovation beginning with and including the excavation of Hell and nexus a part of oblivion for the placement of the new seat of Lucifer's treasury alongside Plautus and Astaroth. This process will begin immediately, and any complaints should be brought to your section chief, where it will be properly reviewed, considered, and discarded and the complainant summarily executed, reincarnated, and executed repeatedly until a proper expression of repentance is expressed in a satisfactory manner. This is Hell.
>
> Nefariously yours,
> Abbadon
> King of Locusts, Regent to the Frozen One

One of the mightiest of the fallen sat at his desk, taken aback at the notice that would introduce chaos of the spiritual kind into his hated/loved Hell.

"What is Management thinking to release such a notice? Do they not understand the rebellion this would encourage?" Samgina vented to his assistant, Amayon.

Bowing, Amayon protested, "My lord, it is not our place to question the edicts of the Supervisor."

Samgina stared at Amayon, who cowered under the glare. "First, do not ever tell me what I can and cannot do. Second, we are bound to speak out against that which might bring damage to our domain. And third, never tell me what I can and cannot do, understand?" Samgina spoke with a quietness that preceded a storm.

Amayon bowed vigorously. "Yes, my lord, it was only—"

Samgina raised his hand. "Okay, stop. All that bowing is unnecessary. Also, there is only one lord here, and that is Lucifer. You may address me as sire or Samgina. Understood?"

Amayon nodded in compliance. "Shall we respond to Lord Abbadon, Sire?" Amayon asked.

Samgina nodded. "Indeed, I shall," Samgina confirmed. Samgina strolled over to his writing desk, sat, and began writing. What all knew in Hell but few appreciated to its fullest extent was that when Lucifer rose up against the Creator, beside him were the angel Perdition and a relatively young angel named Samgina. Though young, he was a spawn of the aspect of Lucifer named Sameal and the archangel Uriel. In the time that Lucifer denied bowing to the Creator's newest creation, Adam, as Sameal, who posed as a snake, tempted Eve, angering the Creator, the one who would be later called the Chairman bound Samgina and Lucifer to Perdition, who was transmuted into a bolt of lightning and cast into what would become Hell. The Chairman then ordered Micheal, his general, to bind the wrathful tempting aspect of Lucifer (Satan) and the Tempter (Sameal) and cast them along with their rebellious brethren to Hell.

To: Abbadon, King of Locusts
Re: Proposed expansion of the realm

My lord,

It appears to us in the lower provinces that very little consideration has been given to this expansion idea. Does *the Supervisor* realize that excavating into oblivion has never been attempted and the consequences could be catastrophic? Beside chaotic seepage, there is the possibility of distortions in reality that could potentially rip this dimension asunder. We would ask for a serious reconsideration of your proposal, and I am confident a solution will be reached that would be satisfactory to all parties involved.

Yours eternally,
Samgina
Marquis, Distributor of the Dead (Materials)

From: The Desk of Abbadon, King of the Bottomless Pit
To: His ignoble marquis (distributor)

Your concern has been noted and considered inflammatory; however, due to our proclivities to avoid the wrath of Upper Management, your letter has been sent forward for further consideration, possible implementation, or punitive action.

Yours questionably,
Abbadon
King of bottom less pit.

Abbadon snickered as he sent for an infernal messenger. "Let's see how the mighty Samgina handles this."

From: The Desk of Ibliss, Lord of Fire, Personal Assistant of Lucifer
To: All provinces

It has been brought to the attention of the most infernal that some have fallen under the delusion that Perdition runs under a democratic process.

Allow us to dispel this most foolish of notions. The King of Evil has set forth clear instructions regarding the renovation and excavation of Hell. Any and all resistance shall be deemed an act of malicious disobedience and dealt with severely. The following shall be the floor plan followed to the letter on pain of death, resurrection, torment, death again, resurrection, so on and so forth, until the proper deference and reverence are believably displayed.

We sincerely think this letter to be of sufficient display to reveal the intent of Management and the expectation of immediate compliance. As incongruent as it sounds, have a pleasant eternity.

The offices of information was run by an angel named Zophiel. This angel/demon had the unique position of serving both the Chairman and the Supervisor. He agreed and disagreed with both his Creator and his chosen lord. Zophiel did not understand why he could not have unfettered access to both Heaven and Hell. Lucifer was going to exile this abomination to oblivion, and when Zophiel begged the Creator for his existence and a purpose, the Creator and Lucifer agreed upon an office that would serve as the go-between for Heaven and Hell. So began his tenure as chief messenger of the realms. In this particular series of messages, Zophiel saw a tremendous event unfolding, and his office was swamped with errands. One particular message caught his eye and sent a shiver down his back. The previous messages, while disturbing, were pragmatic. This last message though was very disturbing and would rock the very foundations of Hell.

From: The Office of Information—Hell's Public Notice of Deposition

NOTICE OF INTENT: Following his concerns for and lack of preventive measures to avoid chaotic leakage caused by a fracture of Hell's foundations, which caused a dimensional rift, the now former ignoble Marquis Samgina has been forcibly removed from his station to undergo reeducation. His position will be temporarily filled by His Unholiness Prince Egyn of the House of Elios. The department of materials is to begin any repairs needed. All construction will proceed without delay by order of Management.

Astaroth, the royal treasurer, sat in a vast room filled with the riches of the world, tributes of gold, jewels, and rarities that defied description. Astaroth saw the beginning signs of rebellion especially with the deposition of Marquis Samgina. *Perhaps the situation can be taken advantage of,* mused Astaroth.

From: The Desk of Astaroth, Infernal Treasurer
To: His most inglorious sovereign the Lord of Pride, Lucifer

Sire,

The latest calculations evaluated by this office reveals that further expansion will increase costs in material exponentially. At the current rate of consumption, material utilization will exhaust supplies/materials in a mortal decade. This office suggests engaging the services of the nefarious demon clans of Azatoth and Azazel to wreak havoc, pursue, and instigate a war in the mortal world with the prime objective of damning as many souls as possible to remedy our looming material shortage. This shortage is, of course, due to the unexpected directive of the renovation, excavation, and expansion of Hell. This office is attempting to assure the proper resources are available for the successful completion of this directive.

Disrespectfully,
Astaroth
Infernal Treasury Department

With the deposition of Samgina as marquis, the expected turmoil never surfaced as the powerful marquis surprisingly left his position without a power struggle. Three kings—Asmodeus, Malbolge, and Glabrezu (regent)—endorsed the princeling Egyn as his immediate successor (unheard of without a council of kings). The sudden and inexplicable release of damning evidence designed to malign the efforts of Samgina took on a note of insider manipulations. Amayon (Egyn's new regent) inspected the fractures on a load-bearing wall and shook his head. *Damn terrorists almost did too good a job,* he mused quietly.

To: The ignoble marquis Egyn, Materials

My lord,

This is a formal request for a ton of materials above our normal order as a recent rupture beside the River Phlegethon has proven difficult as the nature of the river is\was designed to burn the very fabric of the materials being used to plug\patch any hole, rupture, or tear in the substance of Hell. We formally request a substitute material be found and implemented as soon as possible so as not to incur the wrath of Upper Management.

Yours truly,
Amayon
Deputy Chief of Materials

Amayon knew his request would at the very least be pushed down to the bottom of the pile, Management's way of delaying handling a problem they didn't have an answer to. Amayon decided on a course of action that would either get him demoted or a possible promotion. He would sidestep his benefactor and implore the treasurer himself.

From: The Desk of Egyn, the Marquis of Materials
To: Astaroth, Infernal Treasurer

My lord,

Due to increased demands upon this department, we seek permission and authorization to incorporate and utilize a recent invention of the mortal world to assist in the procurement, management, and appropriate distribution of needed materials. This device will enable our department to operate with increased efficiency as misplaced or miscommunicated requests will be eliminated. We are prepared at this time to set up our own computer service department, increasing productivity exponentially. Upon your approval, the "Evl computing system" will begin functioning, sorting, and distributing materials as needed.

With the deepest disregard, your servant,
Egyn
Marquis of Materials

Astaroth read the letter a second time. Did this marquis not know the dangers he was proposing, inflicting Hell with gadgets mortals had a better understanding of than demons? The potential for rebellion was powerful. Still not wanting to expose himself as one afraid to progress, especially with the Supervisor pushing for change, Astaroth sat and composed a carefully worded response.

From: The Desk of Astaroth, Royal Treasurer

My dear Marquis Egyn,

I have received your request with a certain reluctance. This gadget in which you speak has caused noticeable turmoil in the mortal world. My query would be, What would prevent that from happening here?

Have you considered the ramifications of such a mishap? If such a mishap did occur, what would the fallout effect be?

We noticed in your request this possibility was not addressed to our satisfaction. If you would address this matter and resubmit your request, we at Treasury would give your request due consideration.

Most untruly,
Astaroth,
Treasurer

CHAPTER

2

A demonic messenger left the response from Astaroth on Amayon's desk. Amayon returned from his duties to find the message addressed to the marquis Egyn. Though Samgina would never have allowed Amayon to open a royal dispatch, Egyn was much less demanding. With the following of protocols, considering that and the fact that Amayon never sought permission from Egyn to approach the treasurer Astaroth, Amayon thought it in his best interest to know what the royal treasurer had to say before sharing (or not) the information. Upon reading the disheartening letter, Amayon sat to write his own spin letter and deflect its purpose.

> From: The Desk of Amayon, Deputy Chief of Materials
> To: Egyn, Marquis of Materials
>
> My lord,
>
> We have received word from the treasury, and the response is very unnerving. Please advise immediately as we are falling behind schedule with the misallocation and misappropriation of materials. We fear that the wrath of Upper Management will soon be unleashed upon our unholy selves as said afflictions shall propound negative results. We feel that our new proposed offer can and will ameliorate such a possibility. We strongly request that this is impressed upon the unholy treasurer as no one wishes to suffer

the fate of Samgina, the former marquis and current resident of the master's "reeducation sessions."

Yours unfaithfully,
Amayon
Chief Deputy of Materials

Egyn, the newly appointed marquis of Materials, stepped around a worker (damned soul). "See that all my possessions are treated with absolute care, slave!" the marquis demanded. *I'll have this barren waste displaying its importance in Hell's hierarchy,* Egyn mused to himself. "We are the house of collection and distribution, and we shall flamboyantly show our grandiosity with gold and silver mined by the circles that require our goods!" Egyn declared loudly. "We are the depository of souls, and we shall be revered, second only to Lucifer himself!" Egyn shouted, drunk with power. After ranting and shouting for a few more damned souls to get out of his way, Egyn tore open the message from Amayon he'd been carrying. Halting in his tracks, Egyn shook in anger. "How dare he!" Egyn muttered, spun on his heel, and made his way back to his chambers to address Lord Astaroth and demand the reason why such stipulations were being attached to his request.

From: The Desk of Egyn, Marquis of Materials
To: The Dark Lord Astaroth, Treasurer

Sire,

My department informed me of your request. In response to your demands for assurances, please permit our reply that all contingencies have been considered and that this renovation has now escalated to modernization of our beloved-despised infernal residence. That idea being foremost is, we shall be implementing redundancy protocols that would allow for multiple avenues to be readily exploited in case of emergency. With the expectations that this meets your requirement of assurance and full support be attached with your seal of approval.

Infernally,
Egyn
Marquis of Materials

Dark Palace

In the great halls of the Dark Palace, a messenger ran up to the reception desk. "Message for the unholy Astaroth," the messenger told the demonic receptionist.

"His Highness is currently occupied. You may leave the message," she informed.

The messenger shook his head. "I'm sorry, but this is from Prince Egyn, and he demands an immediate answer," the messenger informed her.

The receptionist glared at him with a look that spoke a millennia of arguing with demons. "Listen here, gopher. I don't give a piece of demonic shit who your master is and why he sent your pathetic ass into my office, making demands! When you get an answer is when he gives an answer, not a moment before, you understand that you piece of pig shit!" the receptionist shouted, all the time with her eyes affixed to his, never wavering, never showing doubt or fear. This, of course, made the demon submissive, a trick that worked in the mortal realm as well as in Hell. *Never let them see you sweat,* she thought and returned to her paperwork. After an indeterminate amount of time, the receptionist looked up to see the demon messenger sitting, quietly waiting. "His Lordship will see you now," she announced.

The demon bowed out of deference to this powerful demoness. Upon entering the chambers of the unholy treasurer, the messenger was stunned. Never had it encountered such wealth and finery.

"Stop gawking and be about your business," Astaroth demanded.

The demon nervously approached and handed the message to him, declaring, "From Lord Egyn of the first circle, my lord."

Astaroth snatched the letter and sat to read it. The demon turned to leave. Astaroth snapped his fingers. "No, no, I will have need of you. Sit outside and wait—"

"But, my lord," the messenger interrupted.

Astaroth glared at the unfortunate demon. "Did you say 'But, my lord' as if there is a mitigating circumstance that would validate a direct order, messenger"? Astaroth asked with an edge to his voice.

The demon wondered for a moment how he, in one brief span of time, had gotten himself into trouble with a palace staff member and the treasurer himself. Snapping from his reverie, and with Astaroth glaring at him, the demon wisely responded, "There are no such circumstances, my lord. I await your leisure." Astaroth's stare intensified, making the demon uncomfortable, but the demon maintained his composure.

"Tell us your name, demon," Astaroth ordered.

The demon bowed. "My lord, we are called Marathon of the House of Zophiel."

Astaroth softened his gaze. "We are impressed with your composure, Marathon. You will, as of this moment, become a member of the banner of Astaroth and shall serve us personally and exclusively," Astaroth pronounced.

"But my lord—" Marathon gasped.

Astaroth's glare intensified again. "That is twice you have attempted to circumvent my will, demon!"

Marathon's bow deepen. "My lord, my concern was for Lord Zophiel and his—"

Astaroth held up a jewel-speckled hand. "These things are not of your concern. Do we understand each other?" Astaroth asked.

Marathon bowed again. "We do, my lord."

Astaroth smirked. "Very well, attend my assistant as she has a message for you to deliver."

Marathon gave a quick bow and exited, thinking, *I never wanted to work for these sick, twisted royals, and now a royal of royals has drafted me into his service. This is truly Hell.*

Marathon entered the first circle. Here was where the souls were relegated to their infernal punishments. Formerly run by Samgina of the fallen class, the circle was now the domain of Prince Egyn. The prince was chosen by the House of Elios because he was vain and easy to control. The deposition of Samgina was a plan that had been fomenting for centuries. When the true value of his position was realized, the houses began scheming on how to remove one of the most powerful demons in Hell from his position. It was decided (and implemented) that a series of acts of sabotage would cause a strain on the system, causing enough complaints that Lucifer himself would have to depose Samgina. The plan was given a boost when Lucifer charged the staff of Hell with the orders to renovate. This played right into the rebellious faction's hands as it occupied Lucifer, so he couldn't investigate the allegations of malfeasance and mismanagement. The circle was going under renovation as walls were stripped bare, thrones stripped of their former decorations.

Amayon, Egyn's chief administrator, saw Marathon enter and intercepted him. "How may we be of assistance?" he asked the messenger.

Marathon handed him the message. "A message from Lord Astaroth for His Grace Lord Egyn," Marathon reported.

Amayon frowned. "I am his chief administrator. You may entrust the message to me."

Marathon hesitated a second but produced a tablet. "Sign here as the receiver of this missive, please."

Amayon signed the tablet and dismissed the demon. Going to his desk, Amayon opened the letter and began to read.

From the desk of Astaroth-Infernal treasurer:

My cursed Marquis Egyn,

Having received your letter of assurance, I will, as requested, send your query to Upper Management. However, I cannot at this time add my seal to the said request as your letter, although meeting the standards required, did not meet my personal approval and seemed to be rife with possible ramifications. We at Treasury deem the disadvantages far outweigh the advantages. That being noted, it is not our task here to deem the worthiness of such notions, so your request, as previously indicated, shall be forwarded.

Cautiously yours,
Astaroth
Treasurer

A furious Amayon trembled with disbelief. It was his understanding that Egyn would have tacit compliance with the palace and the other kings, which was why he agreed to betray his former master for an opportunity for advancement. However, it seemed as if the royals were beginning to drag their feet. Amayon would have to think of a solution before handing this letter to Egyn.

In the brilliance that was Heaven, the archangel observed the reports coming into his office via Zophiel's spy network. Irritated by the information, Metatron decided to assure Hell that certain egregious acts would not be overlooked in the renovation.

From the Governing Office of Divinity

From: The Desk of Metatron, the Voice
To: The Supervisor of Hell, Lucifer

Sir,

It has come to the attention of this office that in your recent activities, you have suffered setbacks and damages, which caused leakage of the primordial substance (chaos), and your reported response was to utilize souls for repairs. This action is unacceptable as the consequence is the loss of a soul to the chaotic rift. The *Chairman* is very displeased at such a notion and looks forward to your immediate cessation of this unacceptable practice.

Our second concern is derived from reports stating that your office is seeking to release from Hell instigating spirits with the express purpose of initiating a large-scale mortal conflict to assist in the appropriation of fresh souls with the intention of using them as chaos sealants. The *Chairman* expressly forbids such interference as mortals themselves will bring about cataclysmic events in the very near future, which will assuage any future problems regarding the shortage of materials. We expect *immediate rectification* and *compliance*.

Eternally,
Metatron
The Voice

Metatron signaled for a messenger and an angel from the order of Hermes. "See that this gets to the Dark Palace immediately. The messenger bowed and made his way down Heaven's grand stairway to the Dark Palace, where he went to the receptionist.

The demoness looked up and saw Heaven's glow. She smiled a rare smile. "So good to see you again, Vir-hara. I see your glow is rather warm today," the receptionist teased in a rare moment of friendliness.

Vir-hara blushed. "You derive great joy in teasing me, lady demoness," he acknowledged. It was a fact that innocence could not be found in Hell and that demons easily become enamored by it. "I have a message for the Supervisor directly from the Voice," Vir-hara exclaimed.

"Of course, you do. You wouldn't have come all this way just to visit me now, would you?" Dur-lith teased. Vir-hara simply smiled, knowing never to get into those types of discussions with demons. "Give that to me, and I'll see His Majesty gets it immediately," she assured him.

Vir-hara bowed. "Until next time."

Dur-lith smiled, knowing it would be a while before she had that pleasure again. "I, as always, will eagerly count the moments until then," she teased.

"You never smile for us like that." A passing staff member snickered.

Dur-lith snapped at his heels. "Why in the hell would I inflict pain upon myself for your worthless demon hide?" she growled menacingly. Rising, she walked over to the regent's office and knocked.

"Come," Ibliss ordered.

She walked into the regent's office and handed him the note. "Vir-hara just delivered it from Metatron for His Majesty," Dur-lith dutifully reported. Ibliss nodded, taking the message. As she left the room, Ibliss stood at the door of Lucifer's chambers, awaiting permission to enter.

From: The Desk of His Infernal Majesty Lucifer, Firstborn
To: All parties concerned

We are most displeased at the recent communiqué with the Chairmans office.

It has been brought to our attention that there have been requests from various departments to release instigating spirits upon the world to resolve an issue that was already commanded by yours truly to be addressed. We are furious that permission was not sought through this office to authorize such an endeavor, and the following heads of departments are ordered to report to *His Lowness* with a proper explanation as to why this course was decided upon. The list is as follows:

> Astaroth, infernal treasurer
> Egyn, marquis of Materials

Your presence is demanded immediately!

Yours in wrath,
Lucifer.

From: The Desk of Astaroth, Treasurer
To: Egyn, Marquis of Materials

Your Lowliness,

It was very upsetting to have received a notice from the Supervisor's office due to your request.

We will not accept responsibility for your shortsightedness and are most offended that you got this department involved. Both written and verbal denials will be forthcoming. We expect to see you in due time in the Supervisor's office, where we expect you to give a full accounting on the reluctance of this office to process your request and the admittance that through your personal assurance, this issue would be long resolved per your awareness. Any other issue or false claims made by you or your office will result in an immediate investigation.

Sincerely indisposed,
Astaroth
Infernal Treasurer

Upon completion, Astaroth summoned for his messenger. Upon entering his master's chambers, Astaroth called out. "Marathon, I have another message for you. This goes to the first circle and that effete prince Egyn. Do not allow him to hamper your departure in any fashion. If he claims to have a message for me that he wants you to deliver, advise him that you're my personal messenger and that he should contact the messenger service for himself. We are not about expediting his desires!" Astaroth exclaimed in a short-tempered manner.

"My lord, I am but a messenger. I cannot speak to a member of the royal family in such a manner," Marathon complained.

Astaroth nodded. "I have chosen well with you, Marathon. Normally, you would be correct, but you are not a mere messenger!" Astaroth exclaimed, frowning.

Marathon's confusion deepened. "Have I displeased you, my lord?" he asked, dreading the response. Astaroth reached into his desk as Ibliss stepped into the chambers. Marathon tried to calm himself when the regent entered the room, unsure of what was transpiring. Marathon bowed to Ibliss. "My lord," he said simply in acknowledgment.

Ibliss frowned in response. "You ready?" Astaroth inquired of Ibliss.

Bowing, Ibliss responded, "I bear witness." Marathon kept his eyes on the floor, unsure what to do next. "Marathon, though your service with me has been only recent, I observe in you a loyalty and awareness that is rare. For this reason, you are promoted from messenger to herald of the House of Astaroth with all its privileges and responsibilities. Do you, on pain of exile, from this day forth swear fealty to the House of Astaroth and from this day forward put forth all your enemies to see our house excel in all things nefarious?"

Marathon stood stunned at this turn of events. Slowly he dropped to his knees. "I do swear to follow my lord most loyally."

Astaroth frowned. "I call forth a witness."

Ibliss chimed in, "I Ibliss of the House of Lucifer do hereby bear witness to the enrollment of the former messenger Marathon, now herald of the House of Astaroth.

Marathon frowned deeply and proudly. "My lord, my ignorance notwithstanding, what does this mean?"

Astaroth sneered. "It means that you are my voice. That when you speak in the herald's capacity, you are Astaroth, treasurer to the Supervisor, our lord Lucifer," Astaroth concluded. Marathon stood stunned at the implications. "Be warned, Herald. Do not take the position lightly or become abusive of the power you shall wield. Demons will capitulate to your word, pichas will grovel at your feet, and the damned will faint at your command," Astaroth concluded.

Marathon looked sincere (an impressive trick in Hell where awe, fear, or anger were the emotions most expressed). "I will be mindful and utilize such authority only when absolutely necessary. I thank my lord for his trust," Marathon said, expressing gratitude.

"The only thing you can really trust is if you screw up, you're screwed!" Astaroth warned. "Now, Herald, with your newfound authority, go before kings and say as I directed," Astaroth commanded. Marathon bowed and exited his master's chambers.

CHAPTER

3

Marathon made his way to the first circle next to the great gate Plutonium, the gate of Hell. Atop the ramparts, a legion of demons patrolled. In the air, harpies screeched, and the moans, screams, and wailing could be heard of the damned souls walking, shuffling, and staggering down the now under renovation road to Hell. Marathon thought he heard the snarl of Cerebus. He acknowledged Minos, a great judge in Hell, and turned in the direction of the first circle. Upon entering, he was met by a demon soldier who was on watch.

"I don't recall this circle having guards posted on my last visit," Marathon observed.

The demon looked at the seal of Astaroth branded on Marathon's chest. "I am more like a guide than a guard," the demon responded.

A well-armed guard, Marathon observed.

After a series of passageways, which again Marathon did not recall being there, they entered the first circle. The first thing Marathon noticed was the decor. A mixture of mortal and hellish art decorated the walls. Amayon greeted Marathon and immediately noticed the royal crest. "I see you have tended to your master well, Lord Herald," Amayon observed aloud.

Marathon frowned. "I have Lord Regent."

Amayon frowned. "Yes, well, I'll have that message," Amayon said without the disdain from their previous encounter.

It was Marathon's turn to frown. "I think not, Lord Regent. My master commanded me to deliver this to the lord marquis, not his assistant," Marathon insisted, trying on his royal privilege for the first time and enjoying the fit.

Amayon scowled. "I see you've taken to royal arrogance rather quickly," Amayon observed tartly.

Marathon frowned. "Why yes, quite right. Now if you would." He motioned for Amayon to continue escorting him to the marquis's office. Upon entering the chambers of the marquis of Materials, Marathon saw rare and extinct animal rugs on the floor. Egyn's voice rang out. "My dear messenger, what is of such importance that you could not or, more precisely, would not give my trusted regent whatever message you may be carrying for me?" Marathon approached the marquis, who sat on a golden throne (again new) carved with intricate carvings from the third circle (gluttony) and the second circle (lust). Egyn beamed with pride. "Ah, I see you are admiring the craftsmanship that went into the etchings on my throne."

Marathon looked at the depraved prince. "Just a bit surprised that you didn't have more artwork regarding the works of you own circle," Marathon replied.

Egyn brushed aside the observation. "It could be said that when one aspires for greatness, one should not be content with the mediocre."

Marathon nodded as if in agreement. "Indeed," he responded while taking the message meant for Egyn from his royal pouch and handed it to him. Turning to leave, Egyn snapped his fingers.

"Wait," he commanded. "I would have you return my answer to your master forthwith. Do remove yourself and await my leisure," the marquis ordered.

Marathon took only a moment to remember all that Astaroth had warned him about. Marathon turned to look at Egyn. "How then would it fair you upon the treasurer hearing you had addressed his herald in such a fashion? I'd imagine not well," Marathon passively threatened, which, of course, Egyn took offense to.

"How dare you speak to me in such a manner! Perhaps a proper flogging will see to that arrogance."

Marathon was appalled. He was by no means new to the rules of the court as he served with the Hermes Agency since its inception and had never seen a herald treated so. At that moment, Amayon entered the chambers. "My lord, you have a function you wished done by end of cycle." Amayon sensed the tension he knew would spark between Marathon and Egyn. "Please excuse us, Herald, as my master has much occupying his thoughts with the renovation and all," Amayon said in attempt to defuse the situation.

Egyn, the coward that he was, always looked for the exits and saw the one provided by Amayon. "As you say, Lord Regent," Egyn huffed. "Be then about your business, Herald, as ours is complete," Egyn spat dismissively, returning to shuffling papers around, appearing busy.

Marathon looked at Amayon, who appeared embarrassed (a particularly odd expression on a demon's face). Marathon frowned deeply, almost feeling sorry for him, which expressed itself poorly as Marathon smiled at Amayon, which he, of course, mistranslated and took for an insult. "I'm sure you can find your way out," Amayon said dismissively.

From: The Desk of Egyn, Marquis of Materials
To: Astaroth, Infernal Treasurer

Ignoble sir,

I am unable to convey the depth of my concern and irritation to witness the speed your office has taken in its attempt to distance itself from us upon a mutually agreed-upon plan simply because of the resistance displayed by Upper Management. Your offices and our representatives were well aware of the possibility of such an occurrence and went so far as to develop a contingency plan, which your office agreed upon but abandoned upon the first sign of dissatisfaction. We are bereaved that you would take such actions, and *all* correspondences, meetings, and documented agreements will be brought to any and all forthcoming summons, queries, and/or investigations by the upper-level management.

Furiously,
Egyn
Marquis of Distribution and Materials

Egyn ordered Amayon to summon a messenger then stopped him with a thought. "Amayon, why does the infernal treasurer have a personal courier and I don't?" he asked derisively.

"My lord, the former marquis did not, and since he is the founder of the office, there was none to inherit when you assumed control."

Egyn considered this. "How does that answer my question?" Egyn asked.

Amayon frowned. "It doesn't, my lord. I only await your command." Amayon bowed. Egyn looked like a child receiving a gift. "Let it be so ordered then. Find one worthy to serve the marquis of Materials," Egyn commanded.

A potbellied demon entered the Dark Palace and sauntered to the reception desk where Dur-lith sat. The demon stopped in front of her and waited. Dur-lith observed him waiting and went about her business. After a moment or so, the demon realized he was being ignored. "Excuse me!" he huffed indignantly.

Without looking up, Dur-lith said, "The visitor's restroom can be found down the Hell for further evacuations."

The demon almost staggered under the weight of the insult. (Such bodily functions apply only to mortals and as a painful form of torture). Excretions were very painful, and the damned suffered it regularly). This demoness had the audacity to refer to him as a damned soul! "See here, demoness, you address Nan-yang, personal messenger of the lord prince Egyn, marquis of Materials," he said demeaningly. The bustle of the chamber slowed as other demons keyed in to their argument.

"And what is that supposed to mean to me, messenger boy?" Dur-lith cut to the quick.

Nan-yang trembled with fury. "How dare you!" the fat demon squeaked.

"I have enough dare in me to reach around this desk and beat the fat off of you," she threatened.

Nan-yang was stunned at the audacity of this demoness. "Your actions, behavior, and lack of respect will be documented in my report," Nan-yang threatened.

"Don't forget to report that I called you an embarrassment to anything that carries weight so badly that each shifting of his foot causes a cosmic imbalance." Nan-yang dropped the message on the desk and left, followed by snickering of the staff. Dur-lith picked up the message and brought it to Astaroth's chamber and delivered it.

A loud roar was heard coming from the chambers of the lord treasurer as he read the letter from Egyn. "Give a worm a piece of meat, and he thinks himself a dragon! That insidious toad stool!" he shouted. Staff members began to cringe as the normally even-tempered demon who rarely gave vent to his outrage did so now. With the sound of crashing furniture and the sudden silence that followed, an eeriness filled the air that had the demons of the Dark Palace of Hell frightened.

Marathon emerged from the office that held the messenger's department, doing a brief inspection of the agency that he had suddenly become responsible for being the newly appointed herald of the infernal treasury. Hearing the commotion, Marathon bravely/foolishly walked over to the reception area, where the staff seemed to mill about aimlessly. "Who's in charge here?" he asked.

A minor demon demurely stepped forward. "My lord, that would be you," he choked out.

Marathon quickly closed his gaping mouth and tried to conceal his surprise. "And where is Azatoth, His Lordship's personal assistant?" Marathon asked the demon clerk.

"My lord, palace information is confidential and requires the treasurer's seal to approve such an action," the clerk dutifully reported.

"I see," Marathon observed. "Yes, quite right. I shall await you here while you put forth my petition to Lord Astaroth. If I'm not mistaken, he is in his throne room now. I'll wait here." Marathon took a seat in the small reception area.

The clerk looked horrified. "What am I thinking?" the demon clerk exclaimed, slapping himself in the head in a very mortal-like gesture.

"I don't know. What are you thinking?" Marathon asked, getting impatient with this fool, and wondered if he had he been that obtuse when he was only demon status.

"You are the herald of Lord Astaroth."

Marathon nodded in agreement. "Again, correct," he said with an edge to his voice.

The clerk bowed in deference. "My lord minister, please forgive me. It has been hectic since Lord Azatoth, Lord Astaroth's chief administrator, took leave."

Marathon stood silent, allowing that to work the demon's nerve. The demon bowed nervously again. "But you care for none of that," he correctly observed. He motioned for Marathon to continue. Marathon took a moment, gaze fixed on the clerk. "I would advise you that if you are unsure of a thing, speak not on it." The demon bowed.

Upon entering the treasurer's chambers, Astaroth shouted, "I have an immediate mission that needs doing!"

Marathon bowed. "As you will, my lord," he complied.

Astaroth read the letter then called for the receptionist who delivered it. Dur-lith entered Astaroth's chambers and bowed. "My lord," she said, acknowledging his status.

Astaroth frowned. "Dur-lith, who was it that delivered this, this insult of a letter?"

Dur-lith frowned. "My lord, an effete messenger from the first circle under Prince Egyn," she concluded.

Astaroth considered his receptionist who had served his house since he took position of the infernal treasury. "What was your impression of this messenger?" Astaroth inquired. "Does he measure up to our Marathon?"

Dur-lith shook her head. "My lord, this messenger called himself Nan-yang. He is as his master, full of self-importance," Dur-lith spat out.

Astaroth frowned. "You're giving me the impression you won't think much of him," Astaroth observed.

Dur-lith frowned deeply. "Was I not clear that he left no impression? As he left, the office staff laughed at his callous foolishness, my lord. As I mentioned, he is as the prince who employed him," she concluded.

Astaroth nodded. "Very well. Keep an eye out. I have a feeling the rule of Prince Egyn is going to be a troubling one." Astaroth waved his hand in dismissal. "Do send for Marathon. We have work for him," he called to Dur-lith's retreating figure.

"As you wish, my lord," she acknowledged.

Marathon took what was now becoming a familiar path. Skirting the Gates of Hell, he went along the edge of the first circle and cut back onto a terrace that held the souls for judgment and distribution. It, like the rest of Hell, was being remodeled, although according to rumor, its former ruler was a less flamboyant demon and was said to be of the fallen. Of course, Marathon knew the name Samgina, but it appeared the former marquis was uncharacteristically modest for a demon of such stature, unlike the new occupant of the seat who appeared to take from various circles to decorate his fiefdom— paintings and statues from the second circle (lust), stalls for the gentry of Hell filled with delights from the third circle (gluttony). Marathon was surprised at the speed this marquis managed to decorate his realm considering Lord Lucifer commanded priority for materials. A lower demon approached Marathon as he entered the administration building that was lined and framed by scaffolding. "This is new," Marathon observed aloud.

The approaching demon bowed. "My lord herald, yes, Lord Egyn thought it too austere, too sterile, so he wished to reflect its importance," the demon explained.

"Where is Lord Amayon?" Marathon inquired.

"Apologies, my lord. Lord Amayon is about Lord Egyn's affairs. May I be of service?" the guide asked deferentially.

"You may escort me to Lord Egyn's presence if you wish," Marathon agreed.

The guide bowed. "This way please." Marathon followed the demon to Egyn's chambers, where he was announced. "My lord Egyn, may I present—" The demon was interrupted.

"Very well, I know the herald of Lord Astaroth! What has my brethren have to say to me?" Egyn said pompously. This prince made Marathon's skin itch.

"My lord, a message from Lord Astaroth," Marathon reported, handing him the letter.

Egyn took the letter as if it might bite him. "Won't you join us for some refreshments? As you see, we have the finest from Lord Ghom's domain. Or perhaps you tire from your journeys and would prefer a sample of Lord Asmodeus's wares. He has the best of whores, both mortal and demonic, whatever might be your pleasure," Egyn invited seductively.

Marathon gazed around as if tempted. "Your Lordship is indeed gracious for such a lavish invitation. However, I must regretfully decline as my master has much for me to do," Marathon responded instinctually. He bowed and left. Egyn watched him leave, looked at the letter still in his hand, sat, and tore it open.

From: The Desk of Astaroth, Treasurer

Sir,

Either you did not read or you did not comprehend the terms of our arrangement. If you think Upper Management could cause this highly esteemed office pause for any endeavor it wished to embark upon, you clearly have no true understanding of the prerogatives of this office. No, sir. The demand in which we speak comes from *His Lowness himself.* He is most cross with us, and we imagine you will be receiving your summons for appearance before the dreaded one shortly. We are not impressed with your display of irritation or dismay. Our records as well shall be brought before His Unholiness for his inspection, perusal, and summary judgment.

Yours in spite,
Astaroth
Infernal Treasurer

The Dark Palace

Lucifer sat at his desk, trying (and not successfully, punctuated by the howling of his dark half under chain and string in the ninth circle), to calm his anger over the arrogant marquis of the first circle. *What has gotten into this fool's head?* Lucifer mused. He picked up his quill and began writing.

The message was dropped off by a palace courier. The work around the first circle was a combination of decoration and repair from the incident with the River of Fire. Being supervised by Amayon, the message was given to a junior staff member. The courier gave strict instructions, "This came from the Supervisor himself. I strongly encourage you to see that your master receives this immediately." The staff member nodded vigorously and literally charged into Egyn's chambers, who did not react well to this breech in protocol.

"What is the meaning of this?" he shouted.

The staff member stopped dead in his tracks. "My lord, a message from the Supervisor," the staffer choked out.

Egyn huffed angrily, "Bring it here." The staffer walked up to the throne where Egyn snatched it. "Now begone and never enter my chambers again unannounced," he demanded. The staff member only bowed, wanting to leave as soon as possible. Egyn was becoming increasingly frustrated as obstructions to his goals kept appearing to impede his desires. He sat on his throne and read. Egyn began to tremble at the letter's implications.

> From: The Desk of the Supervisor, Lucifer
> To: Egyn, Marquis of Materials
>
> We find ourselves between the states of confusion and wrath as we ponder the reasoning of Marquis Egyn and why he would feel so entitled as to merit a personal invitation from the Dark Palace when a memo was sent through appropriate channels as to his appearance in our offices. Was it the personal assignment by the treasurer that put the errant thought in the marquis's mind? If so, we would strongly advise dispelling such foolish notions, for if the marquis has forgotten, favor is a curse in Hell, and we do not abide opposable thinking, feelings, or displays of individual grandiosity. It would do you well, sir, to adhere to any summons without reflection as to cause. Immediate obedience is expected upon your next summons. Delay is unacceptable.
>
> Dreadfully yours,
> *The Supervisor*

Egyn glanced around nervously for a forgotten servant or anyone who might be witnessing of Egyn's transformation from confident bearing on arrogance to fear and apprehension after reading the scathing letter from Lucifer. *How can I dispel the notion that I meant to be assuming?* Egyn pondered. Grabbing a quill and paper, he wrote anxiously.

From: The Desk of Egyn, the Marquis of Materials
To: His Most Dreaded Lord Lucifer, Firstborn

My lord,

In no shape, form, or fashion did this office design or attempt to display any contempt at your most majestic rule.

We are most concerned that Your Lordship would think so of us. Our sole wish is to see your demands filled expeditiously and with great quality; however, as you well know, alacrity and quality do not always go hand in hand. Unexpected ruptures and fissures are occurring with disturbing frequency.

If in our zealotry to accomplish your will we have given offense, we blame our desire to meet your expectations and will, in all future endeavors, seek to fulfill your will only as you would have it.

Your servant,
Egyn
Marquis of Materials

The Dark Palace

From: The Desk of the Supervisor
To: Astaroth, Infernal Treasurer
Cc: Egyn, Marquis of Materials

Your presence is requested in the Dark Palace immediately upon receipt of this request.

Abbadon
King of Locusts

From: Egyn, Marquis of Materials
To: Staff

This memo is to inform you that Management will be taking our concerns to Upper Management. We will advise that *all* quotas are met during our absence. *Any infractions* will be met and dealt with harshly.

From: The Desk of Abbadon, King of Locusts (Key Holder)

This is to inform the palace personnel that Astaroth, the infernal treasurer, and Egyn, the marquis of Materials, will soon be attending a meeting with *the Supervisor.* They will be extended all the courtesies of royalty and at all times addressed correctly. *Any* insubordination . . . well, you're in Hell. Are threats necessary?

Dis, Capital City—Throne Room, Dark Palace (Lucifer's Seat of Power)

The Dark Palace was a massive structure that encompassed the sixth into the ninth circle. Tremendous spires thrust up into the vast emptiness between Heaven and Hell. The grounds were a brier patch of differing environments. The hottest part of Hell (the areas that covered the fifth through seventh circles) was where the capital proper was located (between wrath and violence). This was also where Lucifer held court. High demon lords, archdukes, princes, demons, picahs, and the damned could be seen on its streets, going about their hellish business. This region of Hell was dubbed Pandemonium. Named after the god-ling Pan, who was cast down into Hell when he refused to relinquish his old position of deity of merriment. Lucifer convinced Pan that not only would he keep his position but he would also have a city named after him if he would join the ranks of Hell. It did not take Pan long to realize the new deities were not cut from the same cloth, so he joined Lucifer where the father of lies kept his word and afforded Pan a luxurious suite and his own venue to entertain the royalty and those who earned Lucifer's favor.

Egyn arrived at the Dark Palace moments before Astaroth who climbed the steps from his office below the throne room of Lucifer. Draping his narrow shoulders was the skin of an animal long extinct in the mortal world. Accompanied by a small retinue, Egyn ascended the steps to the palace, staring up its tall spires that crowned and flanked the terrifying-looking building. Harpies could be seen and heard flying overhead, screeching, "Woe, woe unto thee! Enter the home of misery!"

This was the grand city of Dis. It bustled with activity appropriate for Hell. Damned souls suffered terrible treatment under the lash of demons that supervised the menial work they were assigned to—everything from cleaning streets, avenues, and boulevards that became immediately filthy again too. Condemned souls (stricter category) had to go into Hell's sewers to clean them out. The modifier being the job is the same as the street crews, except for the fact that the sewer workers had to avoid or fight ravaging demonic creatures that ranged from flesh-eating fish to organ-devouring bacteria. (The dead were given their flesh in this section of Hell from the beginning to the end of their shift and partway into their "rest period," which consisted of a brief time where whatever organism they collected in their shift had ample opportunity to wreak its own havoc on the condemned party.)

A slight shiver of fear made its way down Egyn's back as he realized one mistake could find him in any of these positions. For the first time in his entitled existence, Egyn was frightened. Astaroth reached the top of the staircase as Egyn was passing reception. Egyn looked at Astaroth, who merely glanced and nodded a greeting. *That maleficent beast is going to abandon our cause!* Egyn mused. He quickly followed so as not to be tardy.

CALL TO ORDER: Minutes of meeting between Upper and Midlevel Management

Presided by: Judge Minos
Topic: Renovation/expansion/modernization of Hell and environs
In attendance: Lucifer, Supervisor, King of Hell

> Astaroth, Infernal Treasurer, King of Sheol
> Egyn, Marquis of Materials/Distribution
> Karl Bischoff, Lucifer's personal architect

Minutes as recorded by: Gadreel, watcher

Old business: Lucifer informed the cadre and denizens of the upcoming renovation/modernization of Hell to accommodate the upcoming surge of population.

New business: Lucifer will address concerns regarding new issues brought to his attention. Items include the following:

Material acquisitions
New system of records keeping and department requirements demands
Unrest among cadre as expansion may cause infringement
Questionable policies being enacted without authorization

Recent summons to the Celestial Court in response to a suit brought by former duke Samgina of Materials for unjustified removal of office as stipulated by the Perdition accords

Judge Minos entered the boardroom. Paintings from some of the mortal masters decorated the halls. Seeking favor with the ruler of Hell, they submitted these very beautiful renditions (if somewhat untruthful) with the ulterior motive of lightening their hellish punishments—portraits of Lucifer standing proudly against God during the rebellion, leading his supporters proudly out of Heaven to their new home of Hell. Lies, of course, because there was no glamour to Lucifer's expulsion from Heaven. The artists, of course, were savvy enough not to paint what actually might have happened as opposed to the paintings that massaged Lucifer's pride.

Beldorn, horn of Perdition, called the meeting to order. "Hear ye, hear ye. This is a meeting between the parties of Lucifer, Sovereign Lord of Hell, serving as both petitioned and petitioner, as is Astaroth, Infernal Treasurer, and Egyn, Marquis of Materials. Also in appearance as the petitioner is Samgina, deposed marquis of Materials. Presided by Judge Minos. All deliberations will attend to protocol with Judge Minos's ruling upon the further need of a higher inquiry."

Lucifer shifted in his chair. Judge Minos nodded to Lucifer, who stood. "It has been brought to my attention, belatedly I might add, that certain liberties have been taken without my authorization. Primary is that the execution of Hell's expansion has been met with deliberate attempts to postpone, delay, and even sabotage my desire of the expansion plans."

Judge Minos raised his hand to stop Lucifer before he continued. "If you don't mind, I would like to take this point by point so I don't make a summary judgment but each according to their merit."

Lucifer paused, thinking, *Damn! I forget how impartial Minos can be.* Then he said, "Of course, Your Honor." Lucifer complied with a short nod. "The first topic I'd like to begin with is the renovation itself. Many of my subordinates believe that this is some sort of vanity project I designed for myself out of boredom or something. I assure you nothing can be further from the truth."

Judge Minos nodded in understanding. "And what, sir, is the truth?" Minos inquired.

Lucifer stared at Minos. "I'm not at liberty to say," Lucifer responded acidly.

Minos, unfazed by the master of Hell's stare, stared back. "You do realize I will have to seek verification of this alleged justification." Judge Minos was an old hand and knew when Lucifer spoke in such a manner, it was because the order came from high up.

Lucifer gritted his teeth as his veracity was being put (again) into question. "Of course," he responded through gritted teeth. "We only ask that the inquiry is kept strictly confidential."-

Judge Minos nodded. "It will be given due attention," Judge Minos agreed. Minos motioned to Beldorn, who rose.

"This meeting is adjourned. Please await summoning in the palace's hospitality section as we will adjourn shortly."

CHAPTER

4

Communiqué

J udge Minos retreated to a private room where he sat and made himself comfortable. After a moment, he was in the transcendental state needed to communicate spiritually. He whispered, "Zagan." After a moment (infinitely speaking), an image coalesced.

"Minos, brother, nice to see you," Judge Zagan, magistrate in the highest court in all eternity (the Celestial Court), greeted his demonic kin with the stolid respect that passed as affection among demon-kind.

Minos nodded in respect, returning the greeting. "Brother, forgive the intrusion," Minos began.

Zagan interrupted him, "Minos, you are among the wise that inhabit the demonic realm. If you have a concern, then eternity shares it. What is on your mind?"

Minos gave a short bow as he recognized grace when extended (another way of saying "Look, I know your information is good, but I'm a busy entity, so please get on with it"). "I am currently engaged with the Supervisor who is upset over an apparent disagreement with his staff over the legitimacy of this renovation project and that he is turning Hell upside down. Can you verify his authenticity?" Minos asked.

Judge Zagan nodded. "I can, and I do verify the authenticity of the Supervisor as it aligns with the Chairman's will."

Minos nodded. "Very well then. I thank you for your most valuable time, Zagan."

Zagan nodded sternly. "Be vigilant, brother." Judge Zagan shimmered out as his essence returned to his duties. Minos gathered himself, wondering if Zagan's departing words were a cryptic warning. He returned to the conference room, where the complaining and defending parties returned upon hearing of Minos's return.

Beldorn called the meeting back into order. "With the return of Judge Minos, we reconvene this meeting, allowing for no objections." Beldorn paused, waiting for an objection. None were forthcoming. Beldorn continued, "Hearing none, this meeting is called to order." In the last minutes of the meeting, Lucifer had the floor.

Lucifer stood. "We await the confirmation of Judge Minos as a validation for the source of our calling this meeting to order." Judge Minos stood. "As Lucifer testified, the order for the renovation came from the office of the *Chairman*, so is his infinite authority been ratified in this manner," Minos validated.

Lucifer nodded. "Thank you, Your Honor." Lucifer bowed to Minos, who acknowledged Lucifer then sat back down. "As stated earlier, we are reaching a state of forced postponements as various sects are causing problems for fear of eviction because of the seepage of chaos that has occurred in the newly renovated regions that have accidentally bore into oblivion. We have been commanded to designate certain regions while eliminating any that were redundant," Lucifer stated testily, somewhat upset that he required the Chairman's seal of approval before his own cadre would obey him.

Minos nodded in acknowledgment. "Is there anything else you wish to address at this time?" he asked the lord of darkness.

Lucifer shook his head. "No, but I reserve the right to depose any new complaint you have not yet revealed." Lucifer nearly leered.

Minos cleared his throat. "It is not our intention or our function to hide evidentiary testimony. We are merely following a protocol that has been established by the Celestial Court in order to keep matters fair and impartial. That being said, we will now address the deposition of the former marquis of Materials. We call forth Samgina, former marquis of Materials." Samgina, the dethroned marquis, came forth and sat at the table. "Beldorn, if you would please read the complaint," Minos requested.

Beldorn stood. "That Lucifer, without cause and with malice, did forcibly remove Samgina, the marquis of Materials, from his position of royal damned authority and demoted to a merely damned status," Beldorn read.

Minos turned to Lucifer. "Do you care to respond, sir?"

Lucifer stood. "I find this entire proceeding preposterous as you, Judge Minos, have already found authorization in my application of power as the Alpha himself has given the directive and confirmed it is *not* an ego project to glorify myself."

Minos, somewhat offended at Lucifer's apparent dismissal of his authority, smiled and replied, "May I remind you, sir, the question is no longer your authority regarding the renovation as opposed to the unauthorized removal of a member of infernal royalty, which you yourself had established to assure loyalty from your hosts." Lucifer struggled to contain his fury at such insolence. Minos turned to Samgina. "Do you have a counter-complaint?"

Samgina stood. "Your Honor, it was never my intent to disobey my lord Lucifer. I did, however, feel it was my duty to point out potentially devastating effects if certain issues were not immediately addressed. If you would, I have a copy of the letter I sent to His Lordship outlining my complaint," Samgina concluded. The bailiff walked up to the former marquis and took the memo, handing it to Minos, who began reading it.

Lucifer stood. "Your Honor, that report does not accurately—"

Minos looked up from his reading. "You are aware that I do know how to read, Lord Lucifer?" Minos asked tartly.

Lucifer smiled, realizing that Minos was insulted. "Your Honor, I did not mean to imply that you could not."

Minos stared at Lucifer (being a judge in Heaven or Hell carried a great deal of authority, so much so that even Lucifer would not lock eyes with him). "Is the implication that I would be unable to discern whether this was relevant to the case?" Judge Minos inquired.

Lucifer raised his hands. "Not at all, Your Honor. We beg your pardon for interrupting your contemplation," Lucifer deferred.

After a moment of looking at Lucifer, who was intently looking at his feet, Minos went back to his reading. After a moment, Minos looked up. "Do you have anything else you'd like to present at this time?" Minos asked Samgina.

Samgina shook his head. "No, Your Honor."

Minos motioned to the bailiff. "All rise. We will take a short recess as the judge ascertains his ruling," he announced.

The Dark Palace

Lucifer stormed into the room with smoke (literary) rising up around him. "That goddamned Samgina! I want to find his mother and shove him back where he came from!"

Ibliss, Lucifer's private secretary, ran behind him, ready to write, pick up thrown furniture, or do whatever else the dark king required. "Master, Judge Minos will see the validity of your actions," Ibliss piped, trying to quiet the rage of Lucifer.

Turning sharply to look at Ibliss, Lucifer hissed, "Do you really think that, little one?"

Ibliss froze, knowing this was the manner Lucifer spoke to those who were about to be treated to a nefarious round of demonic appreciation. "My lord," Ibliss began softly, "no one truly knows what goes on in the mind of these judges. They are tainted and try extremely hard to please the Chairman. I am but your lowly assistant. Forgive me for speaking out of place." Ibliss softly pled.

In a rare moment of temperance, Lucifer softly piped at Ibliss, "There is nothing lowly about you, my loyal assistant."

Ibliss bowed. "My lord" was all Ibliss said in response, knowing the rarity of a compliment from Lucifer.

Awaiting his master's dismissal, Ibliss stood. With Lucifer's wave of dismissal, Ibliss bowed out of the presence of his dark master. The palace seemed less frantic than usual. Ibliss accounted that to the suit brought by the angry former marquis. Ibliss continued to his desk.

Talons clicking on the polished black marble floors, Samgina, the former marquis, approached Ibliss, who sat at his desk in Lucifer's reception area. "Hello, Ibliss," the former marquis said in greeting.

Ibliss looked up, pretending to just notice Samgina's presence. "Greetings." Ibliss frowned, revealing needle-sharp fangs.

Samgina returned the leer with a more impressive set of fangs and quipped, "Have things become so lax that the proper greeting of royalty has been dispensed with?"

Ibliss, though small in stature, feared only Lucifer and was not easily intimidated. He stood. "No offense was intended, but until this office receives official documentation to the reinstatement of your infernal royal status, I am not or is any other denizen of Hell required to pay you such deference. Now is there something I may assist you with, demon?" Ibliss concluded coldly.

Samgina nodded in approval. "Well said. Yes, I would like to speak with Lucifer if I may," the former marquis requested.

Ibliss tilted his head. "An odd request as we are awaiting judgment from the courts now, wouldn't you agree?"

Samgina nodded in agreement. "I do. However, I never wanted this rift between our lord and myself," Samgina complained.

Ibliss tilted his head from left to right and back again. "You have a bizarre way of showing your loyalty."

Somewhat repelled by the insect-like inspection of Ibliss, Samgina continued insisting. "All have misunderstood, which left me no recourse. I never doubted Lord Lucifer's authority. I only revealed the folly of excavating into oblivion for more space. I saw the damage the seepage of chaos was having, and I sought only to avoid it," Samgina complained fiercely, so much so that Ibliss nodded.

"I will ask the master to permit your audience, my lord." He bowed, turned and walked to Lucifer's office. Samgina was shocked and very pleased as all in Hell knew that Ibliss was the dragon at the gate and to persuade him was to have a powerful ally. Ibliss approached the massive doors to Lucifer's inner office. He placed his hand on the door and waited. After a few moments, he heard a command.

"Enter." The doors silently swung open. Lucifer sat at a beautiful black mahogany desk, busying himself with floor plans. He was framed by a huge roaring fire and a portrait of the fallen entering the depths that became Hell. Ibliss gazed around the room as had become his habit, enthralled by some of the portraits that Lucifer displayed.

Lucifer cleared his throat loudly, having become accustomed to the display of awe by Ibliss. "What is it?" Lucifer prompted.

Ibliss snapped back to the here and now. "My lord, the former marquis Samgina has come begging an audience with His Unholiness."

Lucifer slowly looked up from his work. "Samgina, you say?" Lucifer asked.

Ibliss nodded "Yes, my lord. He comes begging to speak of his loyalty."

Lucifer glared at Ibliss. "That demon shit-eating worm speaks of loyalty yet brings suit against me? *Me!*" Ibliss avoided eye contact, bowed his head, and wisely remained silent while Lucifer ranted, knowing that after an outburst, Lucifer quickly calmed down and became cruelly calculating. "That worthless piece of ethereal swine droppings! What does he know of loyalty? He is as loyal as a hungry dog with new pups! He'd devour his own testicles if his asshole told him he'd somehow gain an advantage."

Ibliss looked up at that remark. "My lord?" he inquired, unable to resist.

Lucifer turned to him (as Lucifer was pacing behind his desk as he ranted). Lucifer's glare softened, as much as that was possible, and softly laughed. Sitting down, he asked, "And what do you think regarding this change of heart, wise Ibliss?"

Ibliss bowed. "Nefarious one, the conversation I had with the marquis revealed to me that his loyalty is not to his office but to Hell itself."

Lucifer cocked an eyebrow. The flames roaring in the fireplace seemed to quiet itself in anticipation of Ibliss's answer. Ibliss, a direct descendant of Lucifer and Lilith, took notice that the room seemed to have settled into a state of suspense.

"Hell, you say? Not me but Hell?" Lucifer probed.

"Yes, my lord, everything he has said and done, even to risking demotion and exile. I strongly feel this prince should be reinstated, my lord."

Lucifer nodded. "Send him in." Ibliss bowed as he exited.

Samgina casually wandered the waiting room, looking at various portraits depicting various stages of victorious calamities on Earth incited by Hell and its minions—everything from the fall of man in the Garden of Eden, the possession of Cain to slay his poor, innocent brother (Lilith got great joy from that), the temptation of the Israeli to praise the bull god after Moses freed them to the temptation and crucifixion of Christ. Ibliss softly approached the former marquis. "My lord," Ibliss said quietly, "our Lord will see you now."

Samgina looked at Ibliss, nodding. "We thank you, ignoble prince, and your loyalty to Hell shall never be forgotten."

Ibliss bowed. "I thank you for your words, evil one, but you know how impatient our lord can be when kept waiting," Ibliss replied.

"Yes, of course," Samgina responded, giving Ibliss a knowing smile. Samgina strode to the massive black doors. Ibliss watched Samgina's back as he stepped to the doors, hoping the best/worst for this ignoble prince.

The command of enter rang in the hall. Samgina stepped through the doors, and traversing the space between the doors and the desk of Lucifer, Samgina wisely kept his eyes on the floor and kept looking down as he approached the dark lord. Samgina stopped and waited patiently, staring and noticing the designs etched on the floor. Symbols of ancient meanings were inscribed in delicate swirls.

"Samgina," Lucifer said softly, "whatever could be the reason for a private audience with me as we have an unresolved business in the courts?"

Samgina bowed and lifted his head so Lucifer could look at him without Samgina doing the same. "My lord, I have come to beg of you to hear me."

Lucifer peered at him. "Samgina, I find this to be an unusual request. Perhaps that should have been the first thing you attempted as opposed to getting outside parties involved!" Lucifer snapped.

Samgina picked his head up. "My lord, I did just that, and my reports were met with resistance and threats. I wish only to fulfill my duties to you, Sire, as marquis of Materials and regain my infernal royal status.

CHAPTER

5

Egyn paced back and forth in the spacious office that was mysteriously becoming more cramped by the moment. Gravely concerned about his tight schedule and a disturbing rumor that the former marquis was seeking reinstatement had him as anxious as a six-tailed demon in a room of goose-stepping, big-footed angels. A banging on the door made him jump. Angered by his reaction, he shouted, "Who the fuck is banging on my door?"

A groveling demon entered cravenly, whimpering. "A thousand pardons, my lord."

Egyn was relentless. "One! I have one pardon for you. Don't waste it. What is the meaning of this disturbance?" he demanded.

"My lord, as ordered, I bring you the latest damage estimates." The demon visibly shook handing over a report.

Egyn snatched the report and glared at the demon, who remained rooted to his spot. "Well," Egyn demanded, "why are you still here?"

"My lord," the demon answered, bowing, "the report is most disturbing and speaks of a rupture along the excavated area of the Lethe, the spillage and damages that took place."

Egyn tore into the report seeing the section; gauging the damage assessment, his anger soared. He looked at the date of the incident. Egyn slammed the report on his desk. "This was dated the last cycle! Why is it just getting to me?" Egyn demanded.

The demon shrugged his shoulders. "It was the Lethe, my lord," the demon responded cleverly as if that statement explained everything. After a moment of Egyn staring at him, blankly at first and then with increasing anger, the demon understood. "The

Lethe, my lord, the River of Forgetfulness? They simply forgot," he concluded flippantly.

Egyn snapped his fingers, and the demon was consumed by flames of damnation. Screaming, the demon was carried away to his punishment. "I hope your clever humor and arrogant demeanor keep you company," Egyn complained dismissively. "I'll release you shortly if I don't forget."

Nan-yang cut through a path that was becoming worn as passage became more frequent. Feeling more at home as he approached his destination, his thoughts wandered. *One day I shall have residence in this grand place,* he thought as he looked at the Dark Palace. He entered the magnificent building, walked straight to the receptionist desk and dropped off the message, saying only, "From Egyn, marquis of Materials, for Lord Astaroth. See that it is delivered immediately." He spun on his heel and exited. As much as he wished to be there, he knew until he had real clout that that bitch of a receptionist would always look down on him. "What was her name?" he asked himself aloud. *Dur-lith,* he thought. *I shall never forget that name, and in my time, I shall have satisfaction.*

From: The Desk of Egyn, Marquis of Materials
To: Astaroth, Treasurer

Sire,

Disturbing news has reached your servant regarding the rebellious former marquis Samgina, his request for reinstatement to royal status, and possible reassignment to this inglorious position. Dark King, your loyal servant begs clarification so that appropriate measure may be taken. I write to you in acknowledgment of your patronage on my behalf. May this letter find you manipulating things most foul.

Your servant,
Egyn
Marquis of Materials

Nan-yang found himself on a trail that was beginning to take on small nasty inhabitants, carnivorous rodents as well as flesh-eating mutant bat-or birdlike creatures that took to swooping out of the sky. They seemed to be omnivores as Nan-yang watched one consume first a clump of waste and then turned to snap at him. Nan-yang swatted it away, wondering, *Does all Hell need is a semblance of migration for a form of torturous life to embed itself?* Nan-yang came into what was becoming a familiar sight. The terrace of the department of materials was ever changing as its ruler seemed unsure as to how to decorate his domain. The one constant was that it was becoming more lavish. Entering, he dropped the note with reception who looked at him coldly. Nan-yang, in an attempt to foster a sense of partisanship, frowned deeply.

Unflinching the receptionist looked up at him. "Is this urgent?" she asked.

Nan-yang looked somewhat offended. "My dear demoness, that comes from Prince Egyn," Nan-yang quipped snootily.

Dur-hara looked at him and exhaled. "Do you really want to do this? Please be seated. After a brief period a minor messenger approached Nan yang bearing the sign of Astaroth approached Nan-yang handing him a message. His Grace Lord Midas has a message for your master." Angrily Nan-yang snatched the sealed envelope uttering.

"I was just there why didn't he give it to me himself"? He exclaimed reacting in overtures of arrogance. Nan-yang took a seat, reading the message.

> From: The Desk of Midas, Assistant Treasurer
> To: Lord Egyn, Marquis of Materials
>
> My lord,
>
> His Highness finds your letter presumptuous as you entertain the notion that his disfavor of the former marquis somehow distinguishes you as the preferred candidate with his lord's personal approval. Please allow us (or don't) to relieve you of such a burden. Lord Astaroth does *not* in any way consider you an apprentice or any other title casting you in a favored position. Do realize as a denizen of Hell that it is your responsibility to serve when summoned and abdicate

when ordered to. We hope this clarifies any and all matters regarding any future support in case of an order of removal.

May your eternity be excruciating.
Midas
Assistant Treasurer.

"See this is delivered priority!" the messenger finished as Nan-yang folded the message and stuffed it in his messenger pooch. Nan-Yang nodded in acknowledgment and headed back to his master's circle to deliver the message. Upon arrival

Amayon intercepted Nan-yang. "I will take that," he ordered as he took the message from Nan-yang's hand. Unsure of the protocol, Nan-yang surrendered it to the regent. Amayon dismissed him with a wave of his hand and went to his chambers. Amayon plopped himself down on a chair and opened the letter.

From: The Desk of Midas, Assistant Treasurer
To: Lord Egyn, Marquis of Materials

Lord Egyn,

His Lowness finds your letter presumptuous as you entertain the notion that his disfavor of the former marquis somehow distinguishes you as the preferred candidate with his lord's personal approval. Please allow us (or don't) to relieve you of such a burden. Lord Astaroth does *not* in any way consider you an apprentice or any other title casting you in a favored position. Do realize as a denizen of Hell that it is your responsibility to serve when summoned and abdicate when ordered to. We hope this clarifies any and all matters regarding any future support in case of an order of removal.

May your eternity be excruciating.

Midas
Assistant Treasurer

A whimper-like sound escaped his lips. Amayon shook his head as he read the memo delivered by the demon. "This is bad," he whispered. He slowly rose from his desk to go to the marquis's office. He began to consider other placements. Maybe Abbadon needed a good assistant. *We are not that easy to come by,* he mused. He knocked on Egyn's chamber door.

"Enter," boomed a voice within the office.

Amayon smiled as he heard Egyn attempt to replicate Lucifer's commanding voice. *Too much, too little, and much too late,* thought Amayon as he entered.

Egyn seemed nervous, not a good look on a demon, even less so on a demon with power. "Well?" Egyn demanded. Amayon bowed, something Samgina never demanded. Amayon remembered nostalgically. He only wished to remember the reason why he was so quick to betray his former master. "I'm waiting!" Egyn snapped. Amayon had drifted. Snapping back to the present, Amayon cleared his throat to speak, but before he uttered a word, Egyn raised his hand. "Remember well, Amayon, all that I promised and delivered when we overthrew the weakling Samgina. Remember how I've elevated you beyond your peers and how you walk with me in the halls of the nobles," Egyn reminded him.

Amayon bowed, thinking, *Weakling.* Another thing Samgina didn't do was remind the favors he endowed on others. Amayon decided not to speak to this pompous ass, and he handed Egyn the memo from the treasury.

"What's this?" Egyn snapped, snatching the memo. Amayon remained silent, quietly relishing the anguish of uncertainty he had no doubt Egyn would be suffering after reading the note. Much to Amayon's dismay, Egyn's response was unexpected and, to Amayon's understanding, unwarranted. "Well, this is excellent," Egyn whispered. Seeing the blank look on Amayon's face and mistaking it for ignorance, he laughed at his assistant. "Ah, my foolish little helper," Egyn quipped insultingly. "Your unrefined mind cannot grasp the subtle nuance suggested by our nefarious treasurer," Egyn gloated.

Amayon bowed. "Indeed, milord, the subtleties of the nobles escape me. May I beg your teaching, milord?" Amayon feigned, begging.

The arrogant demon prince sniffed disdainfully. "Consider this an education from a superior," Egyn huffed. Amayon wisely remained silent and bowed. "Well, my simpleminded assistant, the treasurer was telling us that if we are to strike, then now must be the time and that in doing so no repercussions would be forthcoming. Have I made this clear for you?" Egyn hissed.

Amayon bowed. "Perfectly, milord. We have been educated by your wisdom." Amayon fawned. Like most demons, compliments were very seductive, and despite himself (or because of his true nature), Egyn found himself feeling flattered and hurriedly dismissed Amayon so as not to give his assistant an advantage—an advantage he had surrendered almost immediately after taking office as his incompetency was glaring and frequently displayed. Amayon hurried from the current marquis's presence. With a mounting sense of dread, Amayon decided to seek independent help. He headed for his chambers.

From: The Desk of Amayon, Assistant to the Marquis of Materials
To: The Desk of Malcoda, Assistant to Malbolge, King of Fraud

Distinguished clansman,

I find myself in a precarious situation as the current marquis of Materials is stunningly incompetent and reliant only upon his ignoble rank in hells hierarchy. He believes he is protected by Treasury and even thinks the treasurer himself watches over him. I implore your assistance at this time as I sense a great upheaval about to occur, and I have no wish to be in the path of the upcoming storm that is about to be unleashed here. Any assistance would have me greatly indebted to you.

In distaste and with great regret, your clansman,
Amayon
Assistant to Egyn, Marquis of Materials

Amayon leaped to his feet as one of his minions burst through the door, shouting hysterically, "Chief! Chief!"

Amayon strode to where the demon imp stood and delivered a vicious slap across the imp's face, silencing him. Amayon stared down at him. "What is it?" he demanded.

The imp began to mutter incoherently again and quickly slowed himself when he saw Amayon raise his hand for another strike. "There has been a breach in the same general region along the Lethe, my lord," the imp reluctantly reported.

Amayon glared with panic in his eyes. "Has Lord Egyn been told yet?"

The imp shook his head. "No, Chief, I came straight to you."

Amayon couldn't help but feel a grudging admiration for the sense of self-preservation the imp class of demons had. Without any supernatural intelligence or cunning or powers, they instinctively knew when to get out of harm's way. Perhaps that was their power, as most demons were either too stupid or arrogant to do what imps did as second nature, step aside and let danger pass. In either case, this particular imp knew the report he just gave was going to have the marquis looking for someone to blame or lash out at. "Very well. Say no more of this, and I shall report it personally," Amayon ordered.

The imp bowed gratefully that the matter would be handled by anyone other than him. When the imp departed, Amayon pulled the letter he had stashed when the imp burst into his office and added, "Situation now critical."

The River Lethe

The yellow river ran between the first circle of purgatory and the terrace that held the department of materials ruled by Prince Egyn. The river, unknown to all, was the first sight of sabotage when the spies of Malbolge infected the area with flesh-eating bacteria. Unfortunately, the spies did not clean up as well as they destroyed. When the first incident occurred under Samgina's watch, he was wise enough to not only investigate but, upon noticing the cause of the rupture, was also able to ascertain the source and reasoning behind such an act. So before abdicating his office, Samgina spread a thin film of the same substance, but it would take longer to do the same damage because of the minimum amount used. While he might have abdicated the office, Samgina knew this would be a protracted event and planned accordingly.

Demons screamed at one another ineffectively as directions or orders were quickly forgotten as the immediate excavation crew was soaked by the River of Forgetfulness. A demon foreman stood over the gap, screaming instructions, "Get me some more sealant and get that goddamned rupture patched up! And try not to get yourselves wet for the hate of Lucifer!" The demons struggled to stop the gaping hole that penetrated into the void of chaos. Some began wandering aimlessly as despite the foreman's directive, they found themselves getting wet. Some demons came running up to the foreman, carrying sacks that, when jostled roughly, emitted moans.

"Get that sealant down there quickly before someone notices what you're carrying!" the foreman shouted at the minions. After yanking out a few babbling demons from the gap, the repair crew finally stopped the rupture that was spewing river water.

"Hey, Chief, you may wanna take a look at this!" one of the repair crew shouted.

Climbing down the hole, mindful of the puddles yet to be mopped up, the section chief made his way to one of the repair crew. "Yeah, what is it?" he asked gruffly. The repair demon pointed to an odd-looking tear in the cavern wall. "What the hell is that?" he asked, confounded.

"We used to use this bacteria to create illness on the mortal world. Here, it acts as a solvent that eats away at anything it's exposed to for an extended amount of time," the repair demon reported.

The section chief looked confused. "I don't understand what you're hinting at," he admitted.

"What I'm saying is that this was put here as an act of sabotage," the repair demon informed him.

"Sabotage?" the section chief repeated disbelievingly. A feeling of dread came over him. "Get this mess cleaned up and make sure that there isn't any more of this shit in this work area," he demanded.

CHAPTER

6

A mayon sat at his desk with a pen in hand, not sure how to write this letter. Actually, it was two letters he had to write, and both were of a nature that could threaten his existence if a slight was taken as an offense. The problem for Amayon was that he quietly helped depose a most ignoble marquis for a cowardly opportunist (odd how even in Hell, like could still attract like) who did not have the devious cunning to run a fiefdom adequately (the perfect patsy for the ambitious Amayon).

Who would have thought it possible for him to have climbed the ranks as he did being such an imbecile? Amayon mused. A knock on his door snapped his attention back to the moment. "Come in," he called. A section chief walked in with his head bowed and visibly shaken. "What is it?" Amayon asked, becoming concerned.

"My lord, the rupture looks like sabotage," the section chief reported.

Amayon plopped down in his chair. "I was afraid of this," he muttered.

The section chief looked at his superior. "What the hell is going on?" he asked, frightened for himself and his clansmen. It was through Amayon's plotting that their clan rose to the prominence they currently enjoy. Conversely, any mishap or misfortune for the clan chief would prove equally or more disadvantageous to the rest of the clan.

"It would seem that I underestimated the tenacity, intelligence, and savagery of the former marquis," Amayon responded.

"Samgina?" the section chief asked, somewhat shocked. "But he was, well, almost timid and very quiet," the section chief pointed out.

"Yes, Anon, he did appear to be all those things, but I think now that was by design. Samgina may be the cleverest of demons as his true evil is hidden, unlike most denizens of Hell," Amayon observed, looking at the chief.

"What are we to do?" Anon muttered, trying to hide the fear from revealing itself in his voice.

Amayon glared at his kinsmen. "Say nothing. I am taking steps to avert any disaster from befalling our clan. In the meantime, I want you to take repair crews and inspect all excavation sites for further infestations. I will share the news with Marquis Egyn so we appear to keep along with his dictates," Amayon informed and dismissed his section chief.

Anon bowed. "Lucifer be with you," he cursed as he exited.

Lucifer is with me indeed, thought Amayon.

Dreadfully and with great impatience, Amayon, assistant to the present marquis of Materials, summoned Nan-yang. Amayon handed him the message. "See this gets to Malcoda, the assistant to Malbolge. Is that understood?"

Nan-yang bowed. "The lord Malcoda, yes, my lord," Nan-yang concurred.

Amayon glared at the demon. "Let me clarify. Not the staff, not reception, the assistant himself. Understood?" Nan-yang nodded and bowed as he left the room. *This had better work, or my entire clan faces destruction,* Amayon thought to himself.

Nan-yang made his way through what was becoming a well-worn path that was started by the herald Marathon. Nan-yang swung at a swooping bat and continued to the terrace of Materials. Upon entering the building, he walked up to the reception desk and frowned at the receptionist. Dur-lith who looked up and rolled her eyes upon seeing who it was. "You again?" she observed disdainfully. "Lord Astaroth is currently engaged, and there is no—"

Nan-yang interrupted her. "Actually, my dear demoness, I'm here to see Lord Malcoda," he said in clarification.

Dur-lith looked up in curiosity. "Please be seated, and I'll inform him of your request," she said politely.

After a moment, he was summoned into the office of the assistant to the infernal treasury of Hell. Malcoda looked the part as he was bedecked in finery. Gold and diamonds reflected the magenta coloring of its environment. "What can I do to you?" the assistant teased.

Nan-yang, who had no ear for such things, went right to his point. "My lord, I am a messenger from His Lordship the regent of Materials Amayon, and he directed me here with a message for your eyes only," Nan-yang reported dramatically.

"Very well then. Give it to me and be seated in the reception area to await my response," Malcoda ordered. Nan-yang bowed and exited. Malcoda opened the letter and began reading.

> From: The Desk of Amayon, Assistant to Egyn, Marquis of Materials
> To: Malcoda, Assistant to Malbolge, King of Fraud
>
> My devious kin of the Mal clan,
>
> It pains me to write you in such a state of distress as we of the Ama clan is soon to come under tremendous antagonism as the failures of the present marquis will undergo extensive scrutiny from the Supervisor's office for unreported infringements, misappropriations, misconduct, and outright theft of valued materials. Because of our shared filial ties, I thought it prudent to inform you before going to the marquis and reporting an act of sabotage by one so clever as to not had left anything resembling evidence pointing to him but instead to an adversary. It is my intention to resign from my post before the shit hits the fan. As stated in a previous message, we think the Ama clan would prove to be a loyal and beneficial addition to the Mal clan. Together, we could excel at the achievements available to us under this reconstruction mandate we are under.

Malcoda sat to read the letter. Upon seeing the depths of his kinsman's desperation, he thought of an appropriate answer that would not compromise or endanger his position. Satisfied with an approach, he sat and began to write.

From: The Desk of Malcoda, Assistant to Malbolge, King of Fraud
To: the Desk of Amayon, Assistant to Egyn, Marquis of Materials

Ignoble Amayon,

We find it curious that you should be writing to us at this particular time. We did receive your memo and request, and while Malbolge is always looking to expand his influence and fiefdom, we are concerned by the lack of fealty or even acknowledgment from your division. We find it delightful that you're willing and apparently most able to act in a traitorous fashion to your current benefactor. Being assistant to the King of Fraud gives us unfettered records to acts of fraudulence acted by man and demon alike, and your act of betrayal to your former master, the former marquis Samgina, has not gone unnoticed by this office. While His Majesty applauds such acts, you must be aware that such behavior would not be tolerated in our division. That being said, if and when such an event (such as the deposing of the current marquis) should occur, it may be possible that our offices may have a position for an enterprising section chief.

However, His Majesty, with due prudence, has demands that must first be met before such an application could be considered. The demands are as follows: (1) sworn allegiance to the House of Mal, (2) an oath of obedience to the dictates of His Lowness Malbolge, (3) disavow affiliation to the materials division, and (4) the sacrifice of your section chief Anon as a show of faith and obedience. These are the stipulations set forth by His Majesty Malbolge as acceptable conditions for your entry to the House of Malbolge. As a sign of his magnanimous nature, His

Majesty will spare the clan of Ama to do his bidding and revel in your accomplishments.

Yours truly in all things deceitful,
Malcoda
Assistant to Malbolge, King of Fraud.

Samgina's Rise

The courtyards of the Kingdom of Alastor rang with weapons smashing into each other. Samgina paced anxiously, awaiting his servant Samgoul to report on how the mission went. Samgina realized the game he was playing was devious and elaborate—one worthy of a true marquis of Hell. He also realized failure would be catastrophic as his entire clan could be obliterated for such an infraction, but what choice did he have? After discovering Amayon and Egyn's plot to depose him, Samgina did what any intelligent being would do under such an overwhelming force—he abdicated. This action sent ripples through the underworld as Samgina was among Lucifer's demons in the expulsion from Heaven. Samgina was exceedingly clever and never believed in confrontation but instead liked to examine an opponent's weakness and exploit it until the intended victim began to believe in their inadequacies and began making mistakes they never made before due to the prodding and misleading information leaked by Samgina. This was dangerous as he was not only manipulating Amayon and Egyn but was also misleading the Dark Palace with his formal requests of restoration of his title and position, all the while funding a rebellious faction furious of the new mandate regarding the renovation.

Through his spy network, Samgina discovered a duke who was also displeased with the new dictates, so Samgina sent his spies in, and they slowly began fueling the disgruntled minions with rumors. Minions do as their nature demands and began seeking avenues of escape. Enter the spies with a bio-weapon, recruiting the disgruntled demon minions and imps (forgive the redundancy). Samgoul plied the angered demon with images of a grateful clan for taking the initiative they themselves were too frightened to take. By placing the device that was given to them. (Being misled of the potency of the device, the demons were led to believe that all the device would do was cause a minor disruption in the work schedule.)

The demons eagerly took up the task, planted the device, and stupidly (because of the erroneous information regarding the power of the device) set the charge and stepped only a few feet away, wanting to watch the amazing effect his contact said he would see if he dared to wait a moment after detonation. To his surprise and utter dismay, the device had a tremendous charge (as was the plan, no witnesses and all). The recovery/repair crew found bits of tattered clothing and occasional demon chunks cast about by the explosion. Closer inspection by the repair crew revealed the toxic bio-element. It was reported by the cleanup team to the marquis that the explosion was deliberately set and that the act, more likely than not, was one of terrorism.

Samgoul entered his lord's office and stood to wait to be recognized. Samgina spun upon his assistant's entry. He gave Samgoul a hard stare. "Well?" was all he said.

Samgoul allowed a small frown to brush against his fangs. "Exceedingly well" was Samgoul's curt reply.

Samgina clapped his hands together. "Excellent! Was their enough evidence left to unsettle him without incriminating ourselves?" Samgina prodded.

"Indeed," Samgoul replied. "I made sure just enough so that after a day or so of contemplation, he would come to the assumption that you have returned, my lord."

Samgina narrowed his eyes. "We must prepare. Egyn will beg the Dark Palace for an investigation."

"My lord," Samgoul interjected, "the Dark Palace is always receiving requests for investigations into some demonic conflict."

Samgina nodded in agreement. "Part two of the plan starts with a clever letter." Samgina considered a moment and went to his desk.

From: The Desk of Samgina
To: The Dark Palace, His Lordship Lucifer, the Morning Star

My brother,

When you ordered my unjustified dismissal, I, ever obedient, did as commanded. Then I came to find a usurper sitting on my throne with my unfaithful servant as his accomplice. More disturbing then was that I had to watch as his ineptitude and inefficiency turn a very accomplished agency into the laughingstock of the underworld. Underscore that with the rumors and outright fabrication that I was in open rebellion against you.

My lord, do you not remember me? Did we not stand against the high throne in open defiance? And when we rode the lightning to our damnation, did we not do so together? I don't know what I've done or not done to have you so angered. I beg you remember me, my lord, as your loyal servant. Return to me what was heinously taken so that I might once again be a part of thy most noble of causes.

Yours truly,
Samgina
Deposed Marquis of Materials

Samgina sat back and looked over at Samgoul. The assistant looked back at his master with awe in his eyes. "My lord," Samgoul began, "your words are stirring and call to mind the days of glory. I saw you and Lucifer stand in defiance. I saw you as you both rode the lightning." Samgoul swiped at his eyes. Samgina pretended not to see the gesture.

"You like it then?" Samgina asked flippantly.

Samgoul grunted. "Well, if you're just going to fish for praise, it was outstanding, persuasive!"

Samgina looked pleased. "Very well. See that it is sent immediately."

Samgoul bowed. "As you command." Samgoul turned to leave.

"Oh, Samgoul," Samgina called.

Samgoul stopped and turned his head. "My lord?" he asked inquisitively.

"Samgoul, check in on Egyn and Amayon. Let us prepare for their retaliation."

Samgoul bowed. "As you command, Sire." Samgoul spun on his heel with an evil grin, reflecting. *Amayon was a fool to abandon Samgina, who is without a doubt among the wisest of Lucifer's servants. I have the fortune of serving him now, and I shall be richly rewarded for helping the marquis in regaining his seat. Both Egyn and Amayon shall suffer for their betrayal, and I will derive much joy from it.*

The Dark Palace

The palace was very active with its administrators or their messengers running from one office to another. Dur-lith could be heard shrieking at an inept demon trying to successfully navigate around the bureaucracy that was the Dark Palace.

"I don't understand," a novice demon (a damned soul that relinquished his right to a soul cleansing that would eventually make him or her a candidate for redemption and allowed entry into Heaven) complained bitterly.

An assistant receptionist tried to mollify the complaining demon. "If you would just—"

The demon interjected loudly. "Just what? Eat my own shit while standing on my head?" he shouted angrily.

"However did you guess?" Dur-lith stepped in, seeing her staff member being treated disrespectfully.

"What?" asked the astonished demon.

"I said," continued Dur-lith, "how did you guess the initiation that is supposed to be secret?" She hissed.

The demon looked confounded. "Is that a joke?" the demon asked.

Dur-lith smiled deeply. "If you have not noticed, this is Hell. We don't do that here."

The demon was confounded. "That can't be right," he complained. "I came on a suggestion from a fellow demon that the clan of the third circle was where one of my tastes would be most suitable," he argued.

Dur-hara continued smiling. Although the uncommon practice began to hurt her cheeks, it was still well worth putting this piece of arrogant worm dung in his place. "Whatever you've come to understand or misunderstand about joining great houses, the fact is, each one has their own requirements specific to their domain and its idiosyncrasies. Now the House of Ghom belongs to the third circle, that of gluttony. In order to join the house of ever-feast, you must show your ability to consume, and His Lowness King Ghom decided if one is willing to eat their own shit while standing on their head deserved a seat at the table of the gluttonous. So what will it be?" she asked, straight-faced. The demon considered a moment.

Dur-lith glared at the demon. "Thinking is something you should have done before coming here! Do you realize you are standing in one of the busiest spots in the universe, and you want to stand there and contemplate?" she shrieked.

The demon took a deep breath. "No, no, I shall do as King Ghom requires," the demon capitulated. "What room do you wish me to retire to?" he inquired. Dur-lith had to fight the impulse to frown.

"Room? No demon who is a true glutton cares about those who may witness his gluttony. No, you will go to the center of the reception hall and perform your obeisance for all to see so Ghom will know he is receiving a true acolyte," Dur-lith informed him. The demon reluctantly shuffled to the center of the reception, proceeded to stand on his head, began defecting (painful for demons) and commenced to grabbing chunks from his buttocks and eating his own shit. The assistant looked up at Dur-lith, remarking, "This is a vile form of initiation."

Dur-lith frowned, this time sincerely. "What initiation would that be?"

The demoness looked to the demon who was having a very difficult time eating his own feces and back at Dur-lith. "Do you mean . . . ?" Dur-lith spoke quietly.

"No one abuses my staff without suffering my wrath." The assistants beamed at their new hero. "Back to work. Stop gawking at the shit-eating demon," Dur-lith directed.

A sign lit up behind the demon. "I am called Gorgo. You may call me shit eater!"

Laughter in the form of joy was not permitted but in the form of derision or mockery...

Lucifer's Chambers

Lucifer stood poised over his desk, looking at the latest revisions for "the grand renovation," as it was dubbed. Its designer sat nervously yet confident that his revisions would appeal to the Dark Lord. Lucifer looked up from the papers, snapped his fingers, and beckoned for the designer to step forward.

Karl Bischoff, damned soul and chosen by Lucifer (recommended by Glabrezu, lord of treachery and the ninth ring of Hell). Karl had the notoriety of being the designer of the Nazi death camps of the Second World War. The evil genius of such a treacherous mind reached the king of the ninth circle at the height of the Nazi rule, and upon his death, the king of the circle of treachery knew that such evil would be vital at the end of days. His intuition proved correct when Lucifer announced the renovation plans. Waiting for a cycle so Lucifer could attempt and fail, Glabrezu introduced the designer of corporal evil to Lucifer with the guarantee that the dark master of Hell would be pleased by the work of Herr Bischoff.

Frustrated by the abdication of one of his most productive and steadfast servants and further by sudden disruptions of small rebellions and seeming sabotage, Lucifer decided to give Bischoff a chance. "Do well by me, Master Builder, and your damnation will know carnal comforts known only by the elite of Hell. However, your failure will assure you an eternity of torment," Lucifer promised. Now Karl stood in front of the Lord of Evil, confident of his work, and though he worked for a madman once, he never worked with anyone who was the embodiment of malice. Karl would have crapped his pants if didn't hurt so much. Lucifer was pointing at the designs. "What is this?" Lucifer demanded.

Karl bowed. "What exactly do you mean, my lord?" Karl asked nervously.

"What I mean is this!" Lucifer exclaimed, jabbing at the plans with his finger. "Why am I looking at squares? Why have my lands been renamed?"

Karl nodded in understanding. "If I may?" Karl pled. Lucifer stepped back to allow the diminutive man to step in. "I've laid everything down in a grid pattern."

"Why would you do this?" Lucifer demanded. Karl bowed. "My lord, in this pattern, damned souls cannot evade punishment by running his captors in circles. And let's face it, some of the punitive demons do not rank high on the intelligence list and will and do chase their captors in endless circles. However, in a square pattern, the condemned can be cornered, captured, and punished. The square pattern also allows for more organized rallying and governance as former realms now become estates of one realm. There would be but one king, you, Sire. Everyone else would take on the roles of governors, senators, congressmen, and mayors. This bureaucratic system would increase liability among your servants, and accountability would increase, dissuading rebellious factions, as the increase of information will decrease the possibility of secrecy where all rebellions foment," Bischoff explained nervously.

Lucifer slowly nodded. "Yes, I see it. But wouldn't the displeasure of my nobility increase as they see their environs encroached upon or the restrictions being placed on their authority?" Lucifer complained.

Bischoff nodded. "Undoubtedly, but I was informed this was/is a task that is non-negotiable, and Your Lordship's success seemed to outweigh the discomfort of a few demons. As we say, 'This is Hell.'"

Lucifer looked up with a rare frown. "Well said, Herr Bischoff, and quite correct. Let it be known that Herr Karl Bischoff is the master architect, and except if contradicted by me or my assistant, all shall go as directed by him. Ibliss?"

Ibliss stood from where he crouched unseen by Bischoff. "All has been transcribed, Sire. Your will shall be done." Ibliss nodded in agreement.

Lucifer waved his hand in dismissal. "Back to work, Master Builder. My staff is at your disposal. I expect constant updates. Do we understand each other?"

Bischoff nodded in compliance. "As you command, my lord."

Bischoff retired to a beautiful office.

he walked to and retrieved a crystal goblet from an exquisite Jacobean court cupboard, poured a cup of romanee-Conti and retreated to an adjoining workroom. Settling in, Bischoff began the detailed work of his floor plan template. The grand designer of the Nazi death camps had come to his ultimate destiny—to be the designer of the new Hell! He bristled with anticipation and trembled in perverted joy.

CHAPTER

7

A Letter of Contrition

Lucifer entered his plush suite and turned to the piping voice of his assistant, Ibliss. "My lord," Ibliss spoke, "there is a letter for you."

Lucifer turned to face Ibliss. "Why are you bothering me with inconsequential information, Ibliss? You have full authority to open general mail," Lucifer said pointedly.

"My lord, this I think you should be the first to read," Ibliss countered. Lucifer gazed at Ibliss a moment before picking up the letter. Ibliss spoke as Lucifer turned the unsigned letter until his eyes fell on the clan seal on the envelope. "It is from the ignoble deposed marquis Samgina," Ibliss concluded quietly.

Gazing back at Ibliss, Lucifer inquired, "Why did you wait until now to give me this?"

Ibliss shook his head. "My lord, I found it only this moment as you came in."

Lucifer stared at Ibliss. "Things are indeed becoming strange. How is it that this escaped your notice?" Lucifer asked, annoyed at the breech of security.

"I can only assume the House of Sameal is making itself known, my liege." Ibliss bowed at the mention of the ancient lineage.

Lucifer nodded in agreement. "I am not to be disturbed!" Lucifer barked, slowly sitting behind an enormous ruby-encrusted desk. Ibliss bowed his compliance and quietly exited from the throne room, knowing well the position his master now found himself in. The marquis of Materials, Egyn, had powerful allies—powerful enough to successfully carry out a plot to unseat a marquis. That it was Samgina of the House of Sameal was a misfortune that would prove the undoing of Egyn and his crony Amayon. Samgina stood beside Lucifer when he rebelled against Heaven. It was only Lucifer's absence that the act of treason was successful. (Lucifer, at this time, was occupied with an experiment of his he called the black death). Samgina was loyal enough to allow the usurper his moment for fear of the chaos that would erupt in Hell because of splinter factions. Lucifer broke the seal of the letter as Ibliss shut the giant door.

The Master Builder

Karl was bent over his drafting desk, both elated and deeply concerned. He knew the opportunity of an afterlife was before him. Satisfy Lucifer, and his eternity was assured with lavish gifts and after-lifestyle. In Hell, that simply meant that all his vices would be attended to and pampered. Failure, however, was most assuredly an eternity of brutal suffering. As the architect of the Nazi death camps, he had an intimate knowledge of what that meant. Failure was not an option. That and his natural sadistic nature made him brutal and effective, as the demons presently under his command could attest to. Bischoff glanced over the old designs. Seeing so many of what he considered to be flawed, he was amazed this plan was ever approved. Research (in the infernal library) revealed that the nine circles were roughly bored out by the exiled angel Perdition when he was cast from from heaven and slammed into a dimension between the physical and the spiritual worlds and fashioned by the demon Mulciber. *Now that's interesting,* mused Bischoff. *It would appear that Hell was not created by Lucifer but by this angel, but why was he exiled?*

An imp demon shuffled up to Bischoff. "My lord, the master wishes to know if he can provide you with any materials or manpower to help expedite matters."

Bischoff looked at the offensive creature, trying to remember its name. "No. I have all that I need. Perhaps some quiet so I may review the master's demands for his renovations."

The foul creature bowed. "As you wish."

Karl bent over the plans when an epiphany revealed the answer to his most basic question. How do we design Hell to handle the population surge and be even more effective? Perhaps his penchant for being anal-retentive was what got him this position. Humming "Der Anführer liebt mich" ("The Leader Loves Me"), he went to work designing what would be a revolutionary design.

> From: The Desk of Malcoda, Assistant to Malbolge
> To: Amayon, Assistant to Egyn, Marquis of Materials
>
> Amayon,
>
> I write to inform you that a missive from the deposed marquis of Materials has recently been delivered to the Dark Palace. It can only be assumed that it was addressed to Lucifer. This letter of discourtesy is written in mockery over the delicate position you have exposed yourself to. May your house be prepared for the onslaught.
>
> Disrespectfully,
> Malcoda
> Assistant to Malbolge, King of Fraud

Malcoda reread the letter with a mixture of dread and disappointment. The former because they had awakened the fury of one of the fallen. Samgina had stood by Lucifer, counseled him when he took the form of Sameal and tempted Eve. (Most misunderstand and believe that the apple awakened Eve. Well, in a sense, it was the apple of Sameal's snake that tempted and seduced Eve to her fall from grace.) It was Samgina who stood beside Lucifer as the Almighty stripped him of his Sameal persona, formed the rebellious general Perdition into a lightning bolt, cast Lucifer and his generals upon it, and hurled it into the bowels of infinity. The latter reason being it was this very cunning angel his lord went against when he (although covertly) decided to back Egyn in his plot to overthrow the ignoble marquis Samgina. Malbolge knew full well the lineage and resilience of this demon lord.

This is a final attempt to salvage something of my lord's plan to consolidate the territories and department of materials. After all, it was never my lord's plan to leave it in the hands of that incompetent idiot Egyn! No, he was only a means to an end, mused Malcoda. Summoning a demonic courier,

Malcoda handed him the message. "See that Amayon, assistant to Egyn, marquis of Materials, is given this immediately and tell him you await a reply," Malcoda demanded. The demon bowed and took flight. Malcoda watched his messenger depart and hoped Lucifer did not catch wind of any of this.

Fear Awakened

The hand of Amayon trembled, and the letter that he held fluttered as if caught by a breeze. His cramped office felt as if it was closing in on him. Realizing the letter was a subtle warning, Amayon wondered if Malcoda was trying to tell him who was responsible for the acts of terrorism they'd recently suffered, setting their timetable back as well as causing difficulty between Egyn and the Supervisor. "Malcoda can't possibly be right on this. We deposed Samgina in a fashion meant to shame him to never show his face or be around anyone affiliated with Lucifer." (*The Supervisor* was a term engendered by his staff to prevent the over-usage of the term *my lord.*) Amayon began to think they'd grossly underestimated this fallen angel. Samgina had returned with a cold vengeance and meant to reestablish himself and bring low those who deposed him. *And I . . . I shall suffer the worst because I had his trust and betrayed it,* Amayon thought with a mixture of regret and fear. In the distance, the sounds of Hell intruded on his reflections. The screeching of the harpies, the howling of Cerebus, and the moans of the suffering had none of their calming qualities for Amayon, only a harsh reminder of the tune he might be singing very soon if Samgina was successful in his attempts. *I had best inform Egyn. He will not take this well, and he is not renown for his wit, which made me wonder why he was ever chosen for such a task,* the frightened demon mused.

The Dark Palace

Lucifer sat at his ornate desk staring into the flames of his roaring fireplace. The flames, much to Lucifer's chagrin, seemed to show images of him standing beside another demon whose stature he recognized well. Above them with accusation and judgment stood the Alpha, condemning and casting them toward what would become Hell, and the figure was Samgina, who turned his back on the Almighty in an act of defiance even while Lucifer (unable to believe the severity of the Creator's punishment) stood looking at the wrathful Alpha. This act of utter loyalty was repaid to Samgina by being deposed from his seat of power even though he could have contested for the reign of Hell itself. This loyal servant was treated as those in Hell were apt to be. Regardless, now this letter, this letter of contrition, this plea of recollection had Lucifer off-balance, a position that was very unappealing to the Lord of Evil.

"There is nothing to it!" Lucifer declared aloud. "Ibliss," he called out. His assistant came through the giant doors when summoned. Seeing the severity on Lucifer's face, Ibliss only bowed when entering and remained silent, waiting for Lucifer's directive. "Ibliss, I find myself in an awkward position," Lucifer, in a rare moment, confided. "I am honor bound to aid my old ally and yet duty bound to allow whatever occurrence needs to transpire for the benefit of Hell." Ibliss stood quiet, awaiting a signal from Lucifer that it was the moment for input. "Yet," Lucifer continued, "who is to say which has precedence? I am, after, all the master of Hell, and no will but my own should be the final authority!" Lucifer glanced at Ibliss, who took that as a signal to share his view.

"It is as you say, Master. The former marquis, more than anyone here, beside yourself, deserves to rule here. That being said, he is both a potential ally and rival. Perhaps it is time for His Lordship to give some assignments. Take a hiatus to the mortal world to see how it fares, and knowing the tenacity of the former marquis, the issue will get resolved," Ibliss advised.

Lucifer stroked his chin in contemplation at the suggestion Ibliss proffered. "You are indeed wise and farsighted, mighty Ibliss," Lucifer complimented. "Perhaps you are right, but would you be all right with everything that is supposed to be occurring?" Lucifer inquired.

Ibliss cackled. "Frankly, my lord, I suspect once Samgina decides to move, things will happen very swiftly, and I know with his penchant for perfection, whatever needs to be done will get done most quickly with his proclivity for accomplishment."

Lucifer nodded in approval. "Quite right. Keep this quiet from the staff. I will keep my ears attuned to you. Any incident beyond your vast abilities, then summon me," Lucifer concluded. Ibliss bowed and left the Supervisor to his own device.

CHAPTER

8

Betrayal—a Virtue in Hell

S amgina stood gazing at the vast gates of Plutonium, or what mortals called Hell's gates. The road was under major renovation and crew chiefs, their crews of demons who supervised the condemned souls that were damned to their punishments. The damned souls sought furloughs to labor in these work crews, hoping for either a break from their torture or leniency for their contribution. One of the workers tore down an old sign that read "Road to perdition" and put up a new sign claiming it as "Avenue of the damned".

"That's a hell of a door," Samgina mumbled glibly. staring at the great gates.

The twisting road that led back to the River Styx was, of course, always jammed with damned souls, making their way slowly down the newly named Avenue of the damned in near silence and eyes casting wildly about, trying to make sense with mortal perceptions of the fiery landscape. Looking upon the gates of black onyx, this particular group of souls saw a rarity as the Lord of Hell made to depart, and beside him stood a demon that was both terrifying and pleasing, which, of course, made him even more terrifying as it was difficult to look away from that which frightened.

Lucifer turned to Samgina. "You surprise us yet again dark price. I have read your missive". Lucifer paused glaring out at the throng of moaning souls, if any dared look they quickly lowered their gaze. "I shall be gone for a brief period as I want to contemplate this plan to its fullest potential. Now knowing your dislike of ruling, I placed

Malbolge in charge of Hell. I can't imagine you requiring anything of me?" Lucifer inquired, knowing the answer.

Samgina bowed. "Once again, your imagination does you justice, my king."

Lucifer gazed at Samgina, one of the very few who still seemed to have an aspect of Heaven within himself. As incongruous as it seemed, such was the case. He lusted for nothing but order; all the obedience he had for the Alpha was now directed at Lucifer, or more precisely Hell. Lucifer would admit could be an unnerving type of focus. "Don't let things fall apart while I'm gone," Lucifer chided, turning to depart.

Samgina predictably bowed. "As you command." The unintended show had an extensive line of damned souls staring at the spectacle in awe. Samgina turned his attention to the onlookers who tried to immediately avert their gaze at the terrifying demon but found it difficult, and many began screaming, unable to turn away. Samgina grinned a grin that only issued forth more screams of terror as he whispered in a voice that carried torment, "Welcome to Hell. May you suffer exquisitely." And with an echoing cackle, he vanished, leaving lamentations and wailing as the throng was given a small taste of their destiny.

Materializing in his office, which was modest by Hell's standards, Samgina sat at his desk and made his decisions for allocations, being mindful that the districts that required the materials got it as opposed to the demons who considered themselves and their projects a priority. This was the exact reason Lucifer asked Samgina to rule this portion of Hell. Unknown to many, the responsibilities of the marquis's position required that the materials (basically souls) be allocated and distributed to their proper place of punishment, servitude, or if they were really unlucky, utilized as constructive building or patching products. (These souls actually chose themselves for this status as their intractable attitude and utter disregard for repentance qualified that entity as unworthy of sentience.) Every member of the demonic royalty indulged themselves in every vice imaginable, which, of course, was encouraged by the Dark Palace. From damned slaves, too sexual and cruel enslavement, too exquisite chambers and furnishings, all this to assure that the royal demons would stay damned, because in his infinite mercy, the Creator claimed, "Anyone could be saved if they repented."

Samgina was modest by nature, didn't feel the need for worship or any of the trappings of the powerful; instead, he seemed to be of that aspect of creation that conjured nature. Nature's aspect was primarily consideration. Everything within its system had to accommodate and consider the needs of the aspect and act in a fashion that contributed to the grand scheme of its existence, which was to exist. With this aspect, the being acts in accordance with that which benefits the host. In a demon such as Samgina, that meant when even the Alpha acted in a fashion that came into conflict with his essential being, Samgina, much to his dismay, stood beside Lucifer in the time of rebellion. It was that very instinct that warned him that something was wrong when Amayon entered his office with claims that rumors were being spread that the kings Glabrezu (lord of treachery), Nazarick (lord of wrath), and Mammon (lord of greed) had joined in rebellion against Lucifer for making one of the fallen in charge of materials and that only the abdication of this marquis would appease their anger. Samgina gazed at Amayon. "The source of this rumor, you think it valid?"

Amayon bowed. "My lord, all things should be investigated further to establish certainty. By your leave, I would seek to impose such an investigation immediately to confirm or deny such an accusation as we are discussing a good portion of Hell's royal houses," Amayon responded.

Samgina nodded. "Do as you deem necessary to assess the situation," Samgina ordered. Amayon bowed again and left the office. Samgina frowned and retired to his one luxury. A huge chamber was bored out for him when Hell was first fashioned. In the center of the chamber rested a dragon, rescued when the Alpha removed the enchanted animals from the face of the earth during the cleansing (what mortals called the flood). So grateful was the dragon that it bound itself to Samgina.

"What troubles you, brother?" the dragon hissed snakelike.

Samgina looked up at his old companion. "I have been given dire news, brother. According to Amayon, three kings have risen with claims of grievance."

The mighty dragon reared its head back, evincing surprise. "I would call the timing suspect," the dragon observed.

Samgina nodded in agreement. "I concur," Samgina responded.

"Well, now that we are in agreement, the question would be, Why?" the dragon asked, tilting his head in curiosity.

Samgina shook his head. "No, Elan, never why. The more appropriate question is, Who? The why always comes down to power—acquiring, distributing, or applying. It's always power," Samgina insisted.

Elan nodded his massive head. "Fine. Who then?" Elan asked.

"That is something we will ponder during our journey," Samgina responded in answer.

The mighty dragon postured for Samgina to mount him. "Where to?" Elan asked.

"To Alastor in the seventh circle, as he will give me sanctuary while I let this coup unfold without disturbing the new dictates the Supervisor has issued. We shall let it continue to the point of optimum disruption. Then when events are set into motion that will threaten calamity shall we assuage the wrath of the royal houses and mete out swift and terrible vengeance upon those who would seek to promote their aims above Hell itself," Samgina whispered.

Elan bristled at the thought of the fury coursing through this fallen one. Elan took to the air. "Let us be about your business then," he uttered.

"Yes, and while there, we will consider the who and the response, and pray that they have Lucifer's curse behind this blaspheme, for if not, then a fury most unholy shall be unleashed upon the fools," Samgina swore. Elan flew evasively, attracting little attention.

From: The Desk Egyn, Marquis of Materials
To: Malcoda, Assistant to Malbolge

I would thank you if one were warranted, but your office's readiness to disclaim all knowledge of our actions leave us somewhat confused. That said, this notice is to reassure our supporters that all is as expected and is not, as believed by some, the end of this administration, and despite the expected difficulties, this office has regained the losses suffered by the previous administration and will fulfill all obligations. All resources will be delivered as assured.

Any delays will be met with a 5 percent increase in gratuities. Thank you for your continued support.

Amayon looked up from the letter he had just read and recited to Egyn for approval. (Facts be known, this was the first time Amayon consulted Egyn for anything. Egyn was of the mind that royalty should not get their hands dirty and that the menial work should be left to the underlings, much to his detriment.) Egyn stroked a vile-looking scrap of a beard. "Amayon, nothing you said was true," Egyn observed.

Amayon nodded. "Yes, my lord. Being Hell and all, I believe that if we are discovered, we would at least appear to be maintaining form," Amayon argued.

Egyn pondered that a moment. "Yes, so it does. I trust that all incriminating evidence been taken care of then?" Egyn probed.

Amayon bowed. "Yes, my lord. Our biggest concern now is whether lord Samgina will turn to open warfare or if he will continue this guerrilla type of warfare."

Egyn cackled. "Samgina will do nothing. Did you see how quickly he surrendered and abdicated his position? No, Amayon, Samgina is the least of our concerns as far as any outright conflict. What is not beyond him is the guerrilla tactics. Go then to the House of Azor and commission assassins to rid us of the Samgina problem," the Marquis ordered. Amayon dared not contradict his master but knew the method he sought to employ would backfire badly.

> From: The Desk of Sameal, the Shadowed
> To: Samgina, c/o Alastor, King of the Seventh Circle
>
> Lord Alastor,
>
> I send you this message with the understanding that an unexpected visitor shall soon be upon you. Know that despite rumors that have been circulated, I would hold no ill will to the parties who offered hospitality to said visitation. That set aside, please be sure the measure of your influence does not impede the prime directive. As long as this request is honored, I shall find myself too occupied to interdict, intercede, or otherwise

interfere with whatever complaints or requests that may be asked of this office.

Elan flew in a blood-red sky over great battlements. Demon soldiers drilled in precise formations on the parade ground. Elan circled a great tower, and Samgina peered at demons practicing hand-to-hand and weaponed combat. With a great spreading of his wings, Elan set down on an open section of ground. Soldiers rushed up to Samgina, weapons drawn. When they recognized him, they immediately dropped to their knees. "Hail," they said in one voice.

Samgina stopped in his tracks. "Rise, magnificent warriors. It brings us lascivious awe to gaze upon your wicked faces again." They rose and bowed as one. They spun on their heel, slammed the butts of their spears on the ground in concert, and escorted Samgina as an honored guest.

Sanctuary—Circle of Violence

In the great hall of the king of the seventh circle stood statues commemorating great battles. The centerpiece was truly impressive as it depicted the great war in Heaven, where Lucifer, in his rebellious guise of Satan, stood with Azazel, Beelzebub, Aimon, and Samgina, poised at the moment when Lucifer, in his pride, refused to bow before Adam. Sameal, Lucifer's seductive nature, persuaded Eve. Perdition, in his sacrilege, cursed the *Alpha*, and Satan, in his anger, begged banishment as he claimed, "It is better to rule in Hell than serve in Heaven"—a moment forever etched in the memory of every demon that participated in that ill-fated moment of infinity.

"Bring back memories?" Alastor asked sarcastically as he approached.

Samgina nodded in agreement. "Specifically what would have happened if Perdition had not cursed the Creator?" Samgina shared.

Alastor followed his old comrade's gaze. "As have I," Alastor agreed, taking it upon himself to guide his distinguished guest, leading to a receiving chamber.

"Forgive the intrusion, brother," Samgina began.

Alastor hid a wicked frown. "You are indeed troubled to think such terms as forgiveness has value here in Hell," Alastor teased.

"Poor choice of words to be sure. Excuse then if you will the unexpected." Samgina fell silent as Alastor handed him the letter he received from Sameal. Samgina paused before a chair and slowly lowered himself as he began to read the letter. Alastor stood behind his desk, plopped himself into his overstuffed chair, and threw his cloven feet onto his desk while Samgina read and reread the letter. He slowly looked at Alastor, who grinned and leaned forward. "So is it all-out or covert war that we are about?" he asked with a tinge of joy in his voice.

Azor's Domain

From: The Desk of Amayon, Assistant to Egyn, Marquis of Materials
To: Azor, Master of the Eighth Terrace

My lord,

I write you with news of our joint purpose. Our goals are soon within our grasp.

The fallen deposed has retreated into the depths of Hell. Our scouts report that he is in full retreat with his retinue. Our agents await our commands to abduct and exile him to the well of oblivion. We require two full battle legions to accomplish our goal. Your assistance will be richly rewarded as my lord extends *full* control of your domain without interference. After the deposed is exiled, we will make our case for the cessation of expansion with the evidence of unrest in the realm. We, as a combined house, will be in a position to request the removal of the damned soul named Bischoff. It is our contention that said being is solely responsible for the notion of the expansion to escape his due punishment and gain favor with the inglorious Supervisor. With this damned soul properly assigned, the business of Hell may return to a semblance of normalcy. We expect your answer promptly as time is of the essence.

Azor pondered the letter a moment before sending for his assistant. "Grissal!" Azor shouted. A stumpy, powerfully built demon swayed into Azor's chambers, which was decorated with damaged skulls of the dead that died horrid deaths in battle. "Grissal, see that two battle legions are prepared for deployment," Azor demanded.

Grissal bowed and turned to leave. Grissal paused at the chamber doors and spoke without turning. "Is it the deposed we seek?" he inquired.

"What if it is?" Azor shot back heatedly.

"My lord, I wish you would reconsider your choice," Grissal murmured, uncharacteristically subdued.

Azor cackled. "What is this? The mighty Grissal is frightened by a deposed marquis? Find your grit, Demon Commander, as we are soon to be at war. Or do you seek relief from your position as commander?" Azor asked/threatened.

Grissal straightened. "My lord, it is only that this is no ordinary demon we pit ourselves against, not even an ordinary marquis but one of the fallen—one who stood beside Lucifer in the great uprising, in open defiance against the Creator. He was there when the mighty angel Perdition was forced into the form of a lightning bolt where Lucifer and Samgina were put upon and cast into the cosmo's and formed the domain of Hell."

Azor grunted. "Perhaps you are impressed with ancient battles and tall tales of inglorious rapture. We, however, of the new order see a return to the Hell that has stood since the beginning. The question is whether you still desire your position, or would you rather resign your command?" Azor prompted threateningly.

Grissal opened the door. "No, my lord, I only thought I'd be remiss in my duties if I did not remind you of the threat we were about to take on."

Azor snickered. "We thank you for your vigilance. However, we have not delved into any decrepitude that hinders our command. Do we understand each other?" Azor asked with an edge of irritation in his voice.

"We understand perfectly, my lord. We are yours to command," Grissal wisely answered, knowing the insecurities of his master. *Fool doesn't realize that unless we have an overwhelming victory, this may get us banned from the comforts of our position and degrade us to damned soul status or, worse, the Well,* Grissal pondered. He exited to follow the commands of his hellish master.

By Design

Karl Bischoff barked commands at his work crew, which comprised of damned souls as laborers with demonic supervisors.

"These curves must be straightened! The notion of circles is an antiquated one and shall be eradicated to provide the Supervisor easier access to *all* domains. The idea of kings shall be replaced with governing demons, and the circles shall be squared. With this design, we shall increase punitive space, which is the Lordship's ultimate priority and one I shall attain for him!" Bischoff exclaimed dramatically.

"This silly soul is cursed to have the Supervisor's force of will behind him. Otherwise, I'd take his foolish hide and stretch it over a fire-pit and slowly roast him," quibbled a disgruntled demon whose numbers were growing under the tyrannical rule of this weak and powerless soul.

However, this Bischoff slug had the protection of Lucifer himself, and no demon would ever consider doing anything to incur his wrath. Bent over his drafting table, Bischoff stared intently at his design with a nagging feeling that he was overlooking something of vital importance. Bischoff lashed out at the workers around him. "You! Yes, you there!" Bischoff shouted at a demon that had just delivered a load of waste to be transported to a pit that served as a dumping place. The demon looked around to see if Bischoff could be addressing anyone else. Seeing no one, the demon turned. "Yes, you, stupid. Drag your worthless hide here and take these to the waste pit," he commanded.

The demon grumbled under his breath, "This fool shall not always be under the Supervisor's protection, and on that day, he shall know what it means to be damned to Hell."

Karl was the designer of the Nazi concentration camps on Earth during World War II and was the perfect candidate for the job as he had to build not only a prison but also one specifically designed for the torture and execution of prisoners. Upon awakening in Hell upon his demise, the ever-scheming Nazi officer looked for a way to avoid eternal punishment due to him. Hearing Lucifer's need for expansion, Bischoff, whose reputation preceded him, coaxed a demon to get a message to Lucifer that the great Karl Bischoff wished to aid Lucifer in fulfilling his desire. Karl went on to promise the demon that once he was assigned, he would make that demon his number 1 assistant, meaning that lavishness would be his reward. The demon was hooked.

"Shazu," Karl called. The demon assistant hurried to his master's side. "See that the charges are set on the west walls of the seventh circle. Prepare the demon suppression squad for possible protest or, hopefully, revolt," Bischoff leered.

"But, Master, that is the Kingdom of Alastor, and he—"

Bischoff glared at Shazu. "Do I care? We have been mandated by Lucifer himself to accomplish the task of renovation. Do you not have the wherewithal to do that which you have been advanced for? Have I chosen wrong?" Karl quietly threatened.

Shazu bowed. "No, Master, I thought—"

Karl's eyes blazed. "You thought! I did not bring you here to think, Shazu. I lifted you from the House of Pazuzu for a deed you begged to contribute to, and now you appear hesitant. Have I chosen wrong?"

Shazu bowed repeatedly. "No, no, no, Master. All shall be done as you desire."

With eyes still affixed on Shazu, Bischoff reminded him, "It is not my desire being fulfilled. It is Lucifer's. Never forget that."

Seventh Circle, House of Violence

In the great house of Alastor, a great table was set, where the finest warriors of Earth sat. At its head with Alastor and Samgina, were the greatest of warriors sitting as their captains and lieutenants—from Genghis Khan to Alexander the Great and Julius Caesar. Boudicca of England also graced the table. Samgina stood to addressing the throng. "My most fearsome warriors, there is no doubt that no army can stand against the power we possess. However, there is a method that could still ingratiate into our ranks and destroy us, and that is treachery. That being said, I intend to visit the minor house of Formida and seek to enlist his aid. With his help, we could strike terror into the essence of treachery, thereby immobilizing it and making that force useless.

With that house out of the battle, we shall surely be victorious and can reveal to Lucifer what has been taking place since his . . . distraction and enlighten him to the revolt under his hooves." The roar of approval shook the very borders of the circle as the army's sign of encouragement. Samgina clasped the arm of his old comrade. Rising from the table he pardoned himself. "At this time I must continue to assure our victory. Feast well as time for battle is coming upon us". Alastor escorted him to the waiting elan. Samgina leapt upon the back of Elan, and the mighty dragon roared. "I shall return with terror at my heels!" Samgina shouted to the King of violence. The dragon flew off into the last edge of the circle of Alastor, where Formida resided.

The Edge of the Abyss

Lucifer waited (as if *waiting* is the right word when outside the borders of time itself). He was soon accompanied. "Welcome, Metatron," Lucifer addressed the one known as the Voice of God.

"How may I help you, Morning Star?" Metatron asked, using Lucifer's old honorific.

Lucifer showed a rare smile. "Dirty pool old man. You know my pride is ever my weakness."

"A smile crossed Metatron's lips. "Yes, I do. It is only an attempt to assure you I come in goodwill. How may I be of service?" the great angel asked.

Lucifer began to pace. Metatron patiently waited for the Lord of Evil to speak, knowing that Lucifer would die, be reborn, and die again rather than ask for help. Finally, Lucifer froze and whispered, "Hell is in trouble, and our Creator is insistent this deed be done." Lucifer complained. Metatron stared at Lucifer with eyes that gaze upon God, which, of course, discomforted him a bit. "Okay, turn down the star power gaze. It is not my form of Satan complaining. I mean only to say that factions have formed, and soon I shall have some of the mightiest among demon-kind pitch war upon one another. From violence to treachery, and in the middle, the third to ride the Creator's wrath into Hell leads them."

Metatron gazed out into eternity. "Yes, we know and are a bit disappointed you had not resolved that." Metatron fake disappointment.

Lucifer scowled. "You know, for an angel, your manners are very questionable."

Metatron turned back to Lucifer. "Well, according to your last argument with the Creator, 'there's a little bit of you in everyone.'"

Lucifer gazed at Metatron impatiently. "Enough of the banter. What am I to do?" Lucifer asked intently.

Metatron tilted his head and, with a smile, while saying, "Have faith, Morning Star, the Lord's plan will unveil itself. Patience." Metatron disappeared, leaving a frustrated Lucifer.

What kind of an answer is "have faith"? Lucifer thought angrily. Right in the middle of nowhere, the Lord of Evil sat to contemplate his next move.

Seventh Circle—Terrace Border, the House of Terror

Elan circled the nightmarish terrain. Figures slithered, shadows shifted, and figures of horror slunk about. Elan landed loudly, chasing nightmares away. Samgina waited a moment to be sure the figures didn't return. He dismounted and was greeted by Formida himself. "My lord Formida, may I have a word with you?" Samgina asserted.

Formida glared at his visitor. "What would the mighty Samgina be doing in my realm, I wonder," hissed the shadow-shifting demon. "Has he come to chase us closer to the abyss? We are curious as to why you and the mighty Elan come seeking sport of my subjects," Formida posed.

Samgina shook his head in negation. "No, Lord of Terror, I have come seeking your aid," Samgina responded.

Formida barked an evil chuckle. "And why would the third of the fallen require my aid?" Formida pressed.

Samgina saw his chance. "From the moment you rose, we have utilized your service many times with exquisite success, then you were dismissed to these lower regions as an outcast. I say to you that was a disservice to one that provided such magnificent effectiveness," Samgina acknowledged.

Formida grunted. "I need no history lessons from you, fallen one," Formida hissed.

Samgina nodded in agreement. "Of course, you don't. I know you have received the directives of the Supervisor and is beginning to feel the squeeze of the Bischoff plan. Even now, he plans to eliminate the boundaries of the seventh to expand the territories of the sixth circle as a reward for their alliance to their cause."

Formida interrupted, "As you have, deposed Marquis?" Formida seemed to gloat. "Do not assume we are unaware of the support you offered His Majesty to further your own means," Formida spat as if catching Samgina in a contradiction.

Samgina tilted his head as if expressing disappointment. "Indeed. Have I become so sublime that the Lord of Nightmares and those things held secret in the night that he could not unwind the knot in front of him? I as a loyal servant will always support His Majesty in public. It is in private that my true concerns become known to him so that if he sees an error, he has time and privacy to repair it. You want to know the difference between the rebellious faction that rises and us? We would not go to war and destroy our home in doing so for stature," Samgina said pointedly.

Formida growled. "Why then are you here if not to regain your title and bring the war to Hell?" Formida demanded.

"I have Alastor and his armies, but Glabrezu still rules the armies of treachery, and while he does, he could wreak havoc among any army that stands against him," Samgina explained.

"And you wish for my armies of terror to plague him into inaction while you and Alastor engage the other houses that stand against you?" Formida surmised. "Why, fallen one, should we extend such an alliance to you?"

Samgina looked around and saw shadows slowly slink around him, knowing his next response would lead either to an alliance or the tale of how a fallen fought and either destroyed or fell in an attempt to seek that which was taken from him. "Because if you don't aid us and the rebellious faction wins, our domains will be wiped out, and Lucifer will have to capitulate to the new order, bringing the wrath of Heaven down upon Hell for its disobedience. What say you? Join us or no?" Samgina knew he was risking everything with this gambit, but it was all or nothing.

Formida paused. "And if we are victorious, what then?"

Samgina smelled an alliance at hand. "You and your house will be restored to its former glory. You shall have reign again to plague mankind until the end of days. Four traitors shall be left in your care, and those that seek to bring you down shall be laid low themselves," Samgina vowed.

The nightmare grinned painfully, reached into a satchel he had slung over his shoulder, and removed a parchment. Summoning a servant who bent over, making his back available, Formida wrote for a moment, signed it with a flourish, rolled it up, and handed it to Samgina. "For Alastor," Formida directed. Samgina nodded, understanding. Formida clapped his taloned hands together. "Let loose then the dogs of war," Formida hissed. Samgina raised his hand, and the shadow that was Formida raised his in return. Samgina climbed aboard elan who unfolded his mighty wings and took to the tumultuous sky. "We shall look for Elan's flame and roar as a signal to invade!" Formida shouted at the departing dragon.

From: The Desk of Astaroth, Treasurer
To: The denizens and staff of Hell

It has come to the attention of this office that some of the great demonic houses are choosing a path of resistance that shall *not* be met with any form of tolerance or temperance. We at the Dark Palace are most disturbed by recent events. It has come to our attention that the master architect is being met with open hostility and noncompliance. Know that upon Lucifer's return, his full attention on matters concerning the improvement and modernization of our beloved Hell shall be scrutinized for proficiency and competence. Any discrepancy shall be met with harsh penalties that include but not limited to loss of status and privilege. The Supervisor would prefer to keep things status quo while the renovation is in progress. This office will not hesitate to enact due punishments. We hope this condemnation of such activities will quell such events. We are not foolish enough to think it will, so let this be a warning to any houses that you risk your station if such disruptive behavior continues.

Yours in anguish,
Astaroth
Treasurer

CHAPTER

9

Heaven

T he eternal city shone in glory. Metatron awaited the Creator's beckoning. Upon his signal, the mighty angel kneeled before his Maker. "Rise, my good friend," the Creator of all humbly asked. In awe, the one known as the Voice did so. "My lord, Hell is in a state of confusion as many factions have rebelled against Lucifer's rule. Admit-tingly, they do so secretly, but they do nevertheless," Metatron dutifully reported.

The Creator acknowledged his angel's report. "This was to be expected. To think a den of evil would capitulate to anything outside their own desires is foolish. I think Lucifer is more than canny enough to have seen it coming," the Creator of all responded.

Metatron looked troubled. "But why, Lord, has he not taken decisive action against these usurpers?" Metatron urged.

The Creator glowed brighter. "There is a reason I chose Lucifer for this position in which he is so reviled," the Creator nearly whispered. Metatron stood silent, not wishing to disrupt the moment. The Creator's gaze returned to Metatron as if gazing out into eternity, and with that gaze was a focus that even the mighty voice of God had to turn away. "Be that as I will, Lucifer has the subtle measure needed to handle the situation without destroying Hell," the Creator concluded.

Recognizing the dismissal, Metatron bowed as the Alpha faded from his presence. *If Lucifer messed this up, the repercussions would echo throughout eternity, yet the Alpha seemed unconcerned, as if the future was already known,* Metatron pondered. But that was something the Creator avoided as it was once shared with Metatron. *The eye that sees all sometimes becomes blind to that which is before it.*

The Usurper's Dismay

Amayon sat behind his desk, thinking dark schemes with which to confound his nemesis. Egyn's private courier, Nan-yang, burst into the office. "My lord!" the demon shouted hysterically, quickly followed by an agitated assistant.

"Forgive me, Master, he just ran past—" the assistant was complaining before being interrupted.

"My lord," Nan-yang repeated more urgently. "My lord, there has been an explosion in the eighth circle, and King Malbolge has sent an emissary to meet with Marquis Egyn."

Amayon, to his credit, maintained his composure at the dire news. It was not surprising that Malbolge would send someone to express his anger. He would, of course, make a direct connection with the Samgina problem even though nothing had indicated that the deposed marquis had anything to do with it. Amayon paused, realizing he was entertaining a foolish notion to think that Samgina had nothing to do with this attack. That would be folly. Amayon snapped out of his thoughts. "When is he to arrive?" he asked the messenger.

"He is here now, my lord," Nan-yang responded.

Amayon tried to remain calm. "Well, see him in!" he demanded of the assistant. Amayon turned to the demon messenger who had turned to leave. "Your timing leaves much to be desired," he said dismissively. Nan-yang cowered out, grateful that his hide was still intact, and exited quickly. Amayon prepared himself for his guest when the ambassador entered the office. Amayon was shocked to see that the ambassador was no other than the mighty Malcoda, Malbolge's personal assistant. Amayon cringed inwardly, knowing this meeting was going to be dire for the office of Marquis Egyn. "Your Grace, so very kind of you . . ." Amayon was silenced by Malcoda's uplifted hand.

"Spare us the pleasantries, Amayon. This office has much to explain."

Amayon nodded in agreement, knowing any false claims or pretense to convince an agent of fraud was ludicrous. "It is as you say, we have run into unexpected difficulties."

Malcoda slowly raised his head. "Perhaps I didn't hear you clearly. You mean to say that you undertook to usurp the seat of a fallen one, one of the original that stood beside Lucifer and Perdition against the Creator, and you didn't expect? What is it that you didn't expect, Amayon, that such an outrage would be taken lightly? That he would gladly abdicate his seat of power to an imbecile? No, Amayon, this should have not only been expected but also prepared for. My master is very displeased with you, and our troops will be withdrawing from your ranks. As of this moment, you stand without the aid of the eighth. However, if you should garner open support from the other great houses, you may redeem yourself as worthy ally," Malcoda concluded.

Amayon bowed. "I will relay your message to my master."

Malcoda nodded. "See that you do and do so quickly," Malcoda whispered. "It is rumored the exile may have the support of the violent." Malcoda spun and exited Amayon's office.

The odor could have been fear, but a definite stink rose up when Amayon heard that Samgina might have the aid of Alastor. Amayon gave thought to how he was going to inform Egyn of Malbolge's recent decisions. Amayon knew enough of the vain marquis to know that any news that dealt with difficulties was always met with sarcasm, accusation, and derision. Amayon was slowly realizing that he had gotten himself in a position beyond his abilities to manipulate. Knowing that Hell was not a place that tolerated delicacies, he decided his best option now was try to enlist the fifth circle (wrath) currently held in thrall by Nazarick and the fourth circle (greed) ruled by Mammon. "Mammon might present a problem being of the old ways and insists on deference that had fallen out of use. Still, his aid would be invaluable," Amayon considered with rising dread.

Just then, his servant intruded. "Master, His Lordship the marquis was sent a notice," he called while waving a scroll. Amayon snatched the scroll from his servant and broke the seal."

Amayon shot a piercing look. Nan-yang bowed. "Why are you still here?

Be about your business". Amayon said dismissively. Amayon sat to read the letter.

I am confounded as to why I am here and you are not. You do realize that the House of Malbolge is a vital ally in our cause, and his needs should be seen to as if they are our own!

Amayon tore himself away from the letter to regain his composure. Seeing his discomfort, a servant who entered the room to serve Amayon asked, "Master, is there . . ."

Amayon turned slowly. "You may leave now!" he said coldly enough to remind the servant of his status. He went back to reading the letter.

Seeing as I've been here awaiting your return, I shall make my way to a nearby pleasure palace. I expect you to see into the matters at hand here, and by all means, pay our respects to His Majesty King of the eighth.

Royally,
Egyn
Marquis of Materials

Amayon stood for a moment, fuming. This ridiculous message now meant that Amayon would have to go to the eighth domain of Malbolge to correct a situation that he was just warned about by Malcoda. *Well, at least the idiot Egyn will not be there to fuck things up even worse than they already are,* Amayon foolishly thought. He summoned a servant to prepare his mount.

The Eighth Circle, Kingdom of Malbolge (Fraud)

Amayon arrived on his hell steed. The journey was long and exhausting. Not physically, of course, but he had to ride nearly the entire depths of Hell as the marquis's office was located on the first terrace of the first circle. And while other assistants got much better travel and lounging accommodations, Egyn believed the infernal bureau of budgets was an allowance for royalty, and the serving class (lower demons and especially damned souls) should be responsible for their own needs. Thus, Amayon was relegated to a hell stallion, no joke regarding hellish transport. They were fearless and tireless but also uncomfortable on long trips, much of which Amayon's hindquarters could attest to. Upon his approach, he was met by guards as he dismounted to stretch. A guard pointed in a direction away from the city proper and toward a wooded glade. "What you seek you shall find there," He said sounding bored.

Amayon looked in the direction the guard pointed. "You misunderstand. I'm here to—"

The guard pointed again. "What you seek is there. As is your lord," the guard repeated.

Amayon leaped upon the stallion, who sensed great urgency in Amayon, and he was correct because Amayon shook with anticipation over the possible incident the fool Egyn was fomenting with his arrogance. There was an old story that claimed the moment Lucifer, in his pride, refused to bow down to Adam, his entity (because the energy of his fury was so severe), through the act of mitosis, divided into Lucifer, Son of the Morning; Sameal, the Tempter; and Ha Satan, the Accuser. It appeared that it was happening again as Egyn was beside himself with anger that had its roots in terror. At least that was the facade he wore for those around him, but Amayon, knowing Egyn for his true nature, knew that the effete marquis was terrified that this breach damaged the inner sanctum of Malbolge and could cost him a valuable ally, something he could ill afford. Egyn knew that the deposed marquis had risen in fury and was only now realizing the extent of his foolishness for daring to oppose this fallen one.

Amayon and the hell stallion appeared at the top of a rise of a charred hillside when he came upon the scene of Egyn with a whip in his hand, lashing at the damned souls on cleanup detail. A short distance away, Amayon could see Malcoda and his retinue approaching Egyn from the direction of one of their strongholds. Amayon kicked the stallion into motion, wishing Egyn would put the whip down as it made him look petty, and no doubt that was what Malcoda was thinking if he was also seeing it. Unfortunately, Malcoda arrived first as the unseen dips and choke points forced Amayon to seek alternative routes.

Egyn was sounding offended, which was always a bad sign. "What do you mean Lord Malbolge is unavailable at this time?" Egyn demanded of Malcoda, who looked at Egyn contemptuously.

"Would repetition clarify it for you?" Malcoda replied sarcastically.

Egyn stomped. "How dare you speak to me in such a manner, you insolent worm dung!" Malcoda looked amused, grinning a spite-filled smile that only partly revealed the scorn that he felt for this minor royalist.

His entire reputation rested on a questionable event during what the mortals called the black plague. It was rumored that during a plague of flies, Beelzebub (the lord of flies) had run into a powerful exorcist who threatened to cut short his campaign. Egyn, of the House of Elios (a duke of Hell), knew what was going to befall Beelzebub and, utilizing a demon assassin, had the exorcist terminated when he had Beelzebub trapped between a church and a sanctified cemetery. This holy man knew his business and was reciting authoritative incantations of expulsion, which the demon lord was finding difficult to resist. Catching the exorcist unaware, the demon assassin detached from the shadows, sticking a wicked dagger into his back, then disappeared, with Egyn replacing the demon. A theatrical display was played out as the demon shook the dead holy man as if struggling for Beelzebub's benefit. Then Egyn withdrew the blade, stepping away from the falling body, and began fawning over Beelzebub's safety. "Are you safe, my lord?" Egyn asked.

"Yes, but who was he? How did you know?" Beelzebub asked.

Egyn bowed. "I am Prince Egyn of the great ducal house of Elios. As you know, peering into the future is part of the power of my esteemed lord," Egyn explained. Beelzebub nodded. Egyn continued, "He was a zealot that learned some spells, nothing to be of concern any longer, my lord."

Beelzebub gazed at the body again. *Perhaps in his arrogance, he will have found a home in condemnation, and we shall have an opportune moment with him,* Beelzebub pondered. He looked at Egyn. "We are in your debt," he grudgingly admitted before vanishing.

That was the incident that catapulted the ambitious Egyn to a princely status as Beelzebub spoke of his deed at the council of royals. The House of Elios also enjoyed some of the benefits that came with Egyn's status change, although as in all things in Hell, there were unspoken conspiracies.

When Amayon rounded the final bend that separated him from Egyn, the marquis was handing Malcoda a letter. "Oh no!" Amayon's dread bore fruit as with one simple gesture, the executive assistant and ambassador to a king was just demoted to a messenger. Through his fugue of astonishment, he heard the proverbial hammer strike the nail. "Under royal decree, I demand my colleague and ally receive this immediately, and seeing no hands more worthy here than yours . . ." Egyn let hang arrogantly.

Amayon snapped back to the moment and leaped off the stallion and got down on one knee and bowed his head. "My lord Malcoda," he said reverently, hoping to deflect his anger.

Malcoda peered at Amayon, who was debasing himself as he and Malcoda were of equal station, and slowly shook his head. Looking down at Egyn, he whispered, "I take leave of my lord to do his royal bidding. I'm sure Lord Malbolge will be eager to read your letter." He raised his hand and angrily snapped his fingers. He, as well as his entire party, vanished in a cloud of sulfuric smoke. Amayon understood that for what it was, a rebuke of Egyn's rule as his ambassador and executive assistant who had to ride a Hell stallion while the worthy of Malbolge had possessed actual power. Amayon slowly rose.

Egyn, in conceited blindness, shouted, "You've never dropped to your knees for me! Who is your master?"

Amayon mumbled with fury. "Are you so blind that you cannot count the many insults you cast upon an ambassador of Malbolge? His aid is invaluable to our cause," Amayon said pointedly.

Egyn looked insulted. "It would seem that you have convinced yourself that your service is invaluable, is that what you think, Amayon?" Egyn asked with an edge to his voice.

It was at that moment Amayon began to think of ways he could separate himself from this egotistical fool and maintain his now dubious status. The double-edged sword that was Hell was that it was expected of demons to act in evil ways; however, this left those in authority in a state of constant suspicion, which, of course, led to a state of constant tension with a very high turnover rate. On the rare occasions that a loyal demon is found, the attempts to pilfer the servant becomes vicious. Amayon looked at Egyn. "Are you aware of what you just did?"

Egyn looked down, his beak at Amayon. "What type of question is that? Of course, I'm an aware, fool! Are you aware of how insubordinate you've become?" Egyn demanded.

Amayon paused a beat, knowing his position to be tenuous. "My lord, I only wished to point out that you made a messenger of a personal assistant and not just any assistant but our most valued ally," Amayon said softly, trying desperately to conceal his feeling of dread.

Egyn continued his harangue. "Be that as it may, there is a way to communicate with your superiors that permit you to convey your observations while maintaining the proper decorum!" he hissed.

Amayon was finding it difficult to maintain his facade. Amayon looked off in the distance where the formidable gates of the seventh circle stood. The gates of Violentium were second only to the Gates of Hell itself.

Poked with skulls, mouths agape in final screams, drawbridges of bones, a moat of blood filled with grasping hands waiting to pull you into the depths—this circle housed the violent. It was multitiered from accidental yet violent incidents to horrendous acts of mutilation to, finally, the ultimate savagery, which was war. This was the circle of excruciating pain.

CHAPTER

10

The Seventh Circle (Violence), the Kingdom of Alastor

A tower of bones bound by sinew and fortified with muscle tissue pierced the turmoiled skies. The sharp-eyed demon sentry made out a figure in the distance and rang the signal, alerting the city of an approaching party. Alastor, hearing the commotion, prepared for his guests' arrival. A magnificent roar signaled that his guest had arrived. High above, Elan circled the parade ground. Beneath them, an honor guard had formed. Samgina motioned to a spot in the center of the formation, and Elan flew down to it. Landing softly, Samgina dismounted Elan. The sound of thunder sliced the air and grew louder. The formation parted to allow Alastor, riding a huge war chariot, to pass through.

The great King of Violence stopped before Samgina and bowed his head. "My lord, I was concerned about your quest to the realm of nightmares!" Alastor shouted candidly.

Samgina nodded in agreement. "With cause, Your Majesty, the realm of Formida seems akin to chaos. Even the mighty Elan seemed disquieted by the perpetual turmoil that permeates his realm."

Alastor glanced back at Elan, who glared back fiercely at Alastor, who looked away quickly so as not to antagonize him. "He doesn't appear that affected," Alastor observed. Being the king of violence, Alastor was perfectly aware of the havoc Elan could unleash if he chose to. "Let us retire to my chambers, and you can tell me Formida's words."

Samgina reached into a pouch and handed Alastor the letter from Formida. "Read for yourself what the lord of dread has to say." Alastor reached down, taking the letter, signaling Samgina to join him. Samgina made hand gestures at the dragon, who suddenly burst into flight. Alastor turned to look at Samgina.

"I only gestured that we had things to discuss, and he could wait or fly," Samgina explained.

"And they prefer flight?" Alastor asked. Samgina nodded his answer. "Well then." Alastor motioned to a spot beside him on his war chariot. Samgina nodded and joined him. Alastor snapped the reins of his hell rhino, who quickly went into motion as they thundered to his palace.

Upon arrival, Alastor and Samgina retired to his throne room. Motioning for Samgina to make himself comfortable, Alastor sat in a plush chair and tore open the letter Samgina had given him.

> From: Formida, Lord of the Chasm
> To: Alastor, King of Violence, Lord of the Seventh Circle
>
> Your Majesty,
>
> I have had a conversation with one whom we are mutually acquainted. This party has put before me a consideration I think worth exploring. If the message of the said party holds any validity, then we of the House of Shadows would find it most conducive to find ourselves once again allied with your great house to rise for a common goal and its benefits. Know that the messenger has been issued the only executable signal that would motivate this realm into action.
>
> With anticipation,
> Formida
> Lord of the Chasm

Alastor put the letter down, looked up at Samgina, and smiled a malicious smile. "That is a very disturbing tic. What is that?" Samgina teased.

Alastor's smile vanished and was replaced by a grimace. "It was a smile, you ass," Alastor shot back.

Unruffled, Samgina fought his smile. "Yes, whatever that might have been, can we not do it again? You might frighten the children." Samgina gestured to Alastor's warriors, who were about varying tasks. Alastor picked up Formida's letter and smiled again. Samgina pretended to shiver. "Truly horrifying," he quipped.

Alastor mockingly bowed. "Why thank you."

Eighth Circle, Malbolge

Malcoda entered the chamber of his master and knelt. Malbolge looked up from his reports. "Well, what did the effete royal want from us now?" he asked. Malcoda reached inside his robe and handed him the letter Egyn wrote. Malbolge snatched the letter and ripped it open.

> To: Malbolge, King of Fraud, the Eighth Circle
> From: Egyn, Marquis of Materials
>
> Your Majesty,
>
> Due to recent events brought about by the rebellious Samgina, we have both suffered losses that can be attributed only to the rebel. Your ambassador, who, may I add, was very rude and was a disservice to your office, intimated that you were upset at the attack on your gates by the said rebel. While I do comply with your right to be upset, I think it narrow-minded to assign blame to an ally when it is obvious who the perpetrator is. That aside, we may wish to refocus our efforts to be rid of our common irritant so that we may put our original mechanisms back into effect. We await your decision.
>
> Yours in the reestablishments of our royal prerogatives,
> Egyn
> Marquis of Materials

Malbolge threw the letter to the floor. "This marquis is insolent. He must be taught a lesson!" Malbolge roared. "He dares to demote my executive assistant declaring royal prerogatives? This bastard seed of the ignoble Elios makes claim to his title that makes a mockery of that house!" Malbolge fumed.

Malcoda stayed on his knobby knees while his master ranted. "Master, he is still our ally," Malcoda whispered.

Malbolge nodded. "Yes, of course, you are correct. We of the House of Treachery shall wait to see how this unfolds, but mark my words, this arrogant usurper shall know the taste of my wrath for his insolence," Malbolge vowed.

Bischoff's Manor

The square-shaped building was modest, its landscape empty of any decorations. The only thing besides the building was a statue of Lucifer. This simple gesture let all visitors think that Karl's sole allegiance was to Lucifer. The walkway was made of crushed bone and gleamed eerily. Located on the outskirts of Hell's capital of Dis, Karl was never far from his master's summons. Bischoff, former master architect of the Nazi Army and designer of its concentration camps, had risen through the hellish ranks to become its grand designer for the renovation—a task more daunting than he initially thought it would be. Contentious demons and its anarchic system of rank and file (including its division exaggerated by its topographical layout), the demon lords fought claw and fang to maintain their territories, fighting the architect every step of the way. And Karl found out very early to not handle your own difficulties that earned you scorn, something that could initiate loss of status. (The argument being that if a master had to turn to their immediate supervisor to assist him keeping order in his own domain, then he didn't deserve that domain. After all, this is Hell.)

Karl looked over his design. He thought it was his grandest work. It divided some regions and joined others, and because some were perceived redundant, they were obliterated entirely. It was the total obliterations that had the demons concerned. Bischoff thought the domains of Ghom (third circle, gluttony), Asmodeus (second circle, lust), and Mammon (fourth circle, greed) should be joined, with Mammon as king, displacing Ghom and Asmodeus. To say that the kings were very displeased to hear that their individual fiefdoms would now become vassal states was one of many disagreements that sprung up from Bischoff's plans. He also wished to reroute some of the rivers. Bischoff knew he had to build a strong support base if he wished to make a successful presentation to the Supervisor (Lucifer). Karl, shrewd in Hell as he was in life, made many allies in the bowels of Hell, and, by facilitating a momentary decrease of suffering he gained their passive support by passing on information. Karl understood that sufferance was the coin of Hell, and any diminishment of that brought esteem. He also recognized that gaining favor in such a well-established institution as Hell would not come from any cement-minded demon lord who was comfortable with the status quo but rather from the outcast and lowly demons. Of course, not in power but well entrenched, an intrinsic spy system that would render him the information master of Hell, its chief scribe, if you will. He had outwitted and angered Mulciber, Hell's former architect, as well as Asmodeus, who considered himself "Hell's master scribe."

Through his spy network, Bischoff learned of the commands given to *the* Supervisor by *the* Chairman regarding Hell. Karl saw this opportunity and seized it by making sure his name was on the lips of all the servants of the Dark Palace. The whispers of the "great builder of the greatest of Earth's death camps" spread in the depths of Hell. Like swine to the trough, the gossip spread like a disease, which, of course, would be deemed natural, nothing to be suspicious about. It soon reached Lucifer, and he demanded that this master builder be brought before him. While it might not have been Karl's intention, he made powerful enemies, not least of all being the mighty Asmodeus himself.

When Lucifer summoned Karl, he questioned him regarding the design of Hell. Karl respectfully asked to see the current plans, which were immediately provided. Pretending to be taking the matter seriously, Karl finally stopped perusing the plans and stood silent before clucking his tongue loudly. "Well?" demanded Lucifer.

Karl bowed. "Sire, with dread, I share my thoughts," Karl stammered.

Lucifer waved away his concerns. "Speak," he commanded.

Bowing deeper, Bischoff shared his opinion. "Sire, these plans are childish and redundant," Bischoff stated matter-of-factly.

The air quivered, Ibliss entered the chamber, and bowed. "Sire, Mulciber has arrived and insists an audience."

Lucifer looked at Karl. "Are you the master builder they speak of?"

Karl tried being nonchalant. "I do not know who they are or what they are saying, Sire," Karl added falsely.

"It is not smart to lie to the father of lies," Ibliss quietly warned.

Karl, seeing he was playing with literal fire, quickly admitted. "I am Karl Bischoff, builder of the concentration camps of greater Germany," he spat. "I think that I can take your design into a new millennium given an opportunity," Karl quickly added.

"Tell us, Master Builder, your thoughts, but first, allow me to invite the architect of Hell, the fallen angel Mulciber, the one who took to these caverns and cleared Hell and sculpted its foundations."

Mulciber entered, a grotesque, hunch-backed figure and bowed to Lucifer. then fixed blazing eyes on Bischoff. "So you call my designs childish and redundant, do you?" Mulciber growled.

Bischoff, used to dealing with people in power, handled himself well in responding. "An obvious poor choice of words, my lord. I was only pointing out to the fact that with modern man, these types of confinement will find you in a poor position to extinguish any rebellion."

Mulciber looked from Lucifer to Bischoff and back again. "The monkey thinks himself clever!" Mulciber spat.

Karl fought to remain calm. "Shall I show you the flaw in your design?" Karl dared.

Mulciber stared in disbelief that this patch of pond scum dared to confront a demon of the first order. Mulciber laughed scornfully. "Show me, worm, what you perceive as a flaw," Mulciber demanded.

Karl smiled, (rarely seen in Hell and considered an insult). "Let's begin with the pattern," Karl stated.

Mulciber snarled. "Yes, let's. What is wrong with it?"

Karl pointed. "The shapes," he clarified.

Mulciber stared at Karl as if Lucifer was playing a cruel joke on him. "What about the shape, slave?" Mulciber growled. Karl stared at Mulciber, and his smile grew. Mulciber fumed, and Lucifer was amused at the audacity of the mortal. "You do realize that you tempt torture with your insults, don't you, slave?" Mulciber threatened.

Karl bowed. "My lord, I envy the work you've done, but you have done nothing but revile me from the moment you entered without even looking at my work. And I serve Lucifer, not you. If you want my respect, you in turn must show a modicum of the same to me, not because of any reason other than I, too, am a master architect," Karl insisted.

Mulciber looked to Lucifer, who shrugged. "Seems a reasonable enough request," Lucifer conceded.

"What if he's wrong and his work is flawed?" Mulciber demanded.

Lucifer smiled. "Well, then he becomes your play-thing, and you may do with him as you will, within reason, of course."

Mulciber grinned wickedly at Karl, hurling an insult at the upstart. "Begin then and argue yourself into my power," Mulciber threatened.

Karl pointed to the floor design. "The primary shape of Hell is what?" he asked the fallen designer.

"Are you blind, or do you not recognize a circle?" Mulciber quipped.

"To what purpose?" Karl inquired, ignoring the slight.

Mulciber laughed. "So that the damned fools can be chased eternally with nowhere really to run," he gleefully explained.

Karl continued. "And how does that effect demon morale?" Karl asked.

"Who cares?" Mulciber shouted. A flicker of understanding creased Lucifer's brow.

"The Muslims of Mohammed understood," Karl said quietly.

"And what is it that they understood?" Mulciber demanded.

"It is almost impossible to corner a soul in a round room," Lucifer whispered.

"Exactly, Sire," Karl agreed.

Mulciber grunted. "The idea is ludicrous! In the round state, the damned may have hope, which we can cruelly snatch away, increasing their despair."

Lucifer nodded. "There is that to consider."

Karl shook his head in disagreement. "Sire, it says upon the gates to abandon hope. Besides that, have we not had escapees from Hell requiring us to send collecting agents into the mortal realms to recapture them?" Karl pointed out.

"And we succeed in doing so," Mulciber argued.

"At what cost? We risk exposure, and demons, being demons, are very tempted to be about mischief, endangering the uncertainty factor as to Hell's existence among the mortals," Karl pointed out.

Mulciber turned to Lucifer. "Sire—"

Lucifer raised his hand. "No, fallen one, I think the architect Bischoff has a valid point, and we shall proceed as he recommends.

And I expect you to give your full support to see his idea implemented," Lucifer commanded.

Mulciber bowed. "As you command, my lord."

Lucifer nodded, pleased at the outcome of the meeting. "See to it then. I leave you to your work." The Supervisor of Hell vanished in a cloud of sulfuric smoke.

Mulciber turned to Bischoff. "I do not agree with your idea. However, I shall do as commanded. If you require my assistance, focus on my name, and I shall come." Bischoff bowed. "I am indebted to you, mighty one." Mulciber grunted. "Perhaps you will thrive here if you remember your place, mortal." He vanished in a cloud of smoke.

Bischoff rubbed his hands in satisfaction. "Now begins the difficult process of getting the kings to relinquish their domains for the expansion," Karl muttered to himself. "I had best to set up my own staff." Karl whistled for his hell stallion to take him to his quarters so he could peruse the list of available demons for employ.

> From: Karl Bischoff, Master Architect
> To: Egyn, Marquis of Materials
>
> My lord,
>
> As you know, I have been assigned by His Dark Majesty Lucifer to design and supervise the expansion and renovation of the entire domain of Hell. At this time, I find myself in need of staff to implement his will. I request from your office one personal assistant, four personal messengers, a dozen supervising demons, and a legion of damned souls to act as manual labor. As his lord demands immediate results, I am forced to request that you expedite my request to avoid the ire of His Majesty. Your prompt fulfillment of my request shall be a part of my report to His Majesty, assuring both of us ample rewards.
>
> Yours in damnation,
> Karl Bischoff
> Master Designer

Amayon took the letter from a demonic messenger. Seeing the Dark Palace seal, he brought it to Egyn immediately. Upon entering the marquis's chambers, he found him frolicking with a succubus. Clearing his throat to make his presence known, Amayon, concealed his growing spite for the idiot marquis who, much to his chagrin, had supported in the overthrow of this realm's rightful ruler, announced himself. "My lord, an urgent message from the Dark Palace!" he exclaimed loudly to justify his interruption.

Unimpressed by the reasoning, Egyn stood abruptly, sending the succubus sprawling. "Fool, never enter my chambers again without proper permission!" he shouted angrily.

Unperturbed by the expected rant, Amayon continued. "My lord, the letter has the seal of the Dark Palace. Do you not wish to always be the first to know what is on His Majesty's mind?" Amayon countered.

Egyn snatched the letter. "Remember what I said about entering my premise again, servant," Egyn demanded.

Amayon bowed. "As you command, Sire."

Egyn stood at his ornate throne cut from onyx and inlaid with rubies. Egyn sprawled with his leg draped over an arm that bore a stylized scorpion. The juxtaposition of the unsightly Egyn on the beautiful throne made Amayon cringe slightly as he recalled its former occupant and how wickedly glorious he looked. Snapping back to the present, Egyn was grunting over the letter sent by the master builder. "How dare he speak to me in such a fashion," Egyn fumed.

Amayon stared at his lord, confounded by the fact that this effete, almost delicate, obnoxious demon hailed from the nefarious house of Elios, which was the only reason Amayon betrayed his former master, Samgina. (That and the fact that Amayon didn't think the old marquis was doing Hell a service by showing mercy to certain applicants. Amayon believed that Samgina carried too much of Heaven in his soul.) He wished now he had supported anyone but this inflated, self-congratulatory, arrogant waste of demon flesh.

Egyn snapped his fingers in the face of Amayon. "Where are your thoughts, servant?" Egyn asked suspiciously.

"Forgive me, my lord. I was wondering who would dare write a letter to upset you," Amayon quickly responded, realizing that though the current marquis was a fool, the fool didn't trust anyone, and that could be a dangerous vice, it served this fool and was not to be underestimated.

"Take a letter," Egyn demanded.

Amayon bowed. "I shall instruct your scribe to attend you," Amayon responded, bristling.

"Did I ask for a scribe?" Egyn glowered.

Amayon bowed with anger coursing in him. "No, Sire," Amayon conceded.

"We must attend sensitive matters, and I trust no one else to do it right, my dear servant," Egyn whispered.

Amayon saw through the pretense. *Less witnesses, more room for plausible deniability.* Amayon felt a deep fear take root in the pit of his stomach.

> From: Prince Egyn, Marquis of Materials
> To: Karl Bischoff
>
> My dear damned soul,
>
> As you bear the royal seal, your request shall be fulfilled expeditiously as soon as your usage of the royal seal has been authenticated. You must understand the seal is seldom used by a damned soul, so all attempts to validate such a rarity must be implemented. However, once such authorization has been achieved, your order shall be filled in a timely manner.
>
> Prince Egyn
> Marquis of Materials

CHAPTER

11

House of Shadows

The terrace that held the essence and embodiment of terror was covered with a sickly greenish fog. Many sickly forms darted in and out of the shadows. Upon the completion of the fallen's visit, plans were discussed and agreed upon.

The shifting form saw his guests off. His eyes narrowed at their departure. Beside him approached one of his spies. "My lord," the spy announced himself.

Formida looked at the spy. "What have you learned?"

The spy gazed around, assuring privacy. "My lord, all is as the fallen one has claimed. The bastard offspring of the House of Elios has supplanted one of the founders without incident."

Formida contemplated a moment. "There must be something great afoot for him to be allowed this usurpation without resistance. What could that be?" Formed wondered aloud.

"My lord, reports indicate that many are displeased with the new dictates issued by the Dark Palace. Some even whisper of a grand rebellion."

Formida looked disturbed. "Do they believe the Supervisor incompetent?" he asked disbelievingly.

The spy shook his head. "My reports indicate displeasure over the renovation and possible displacements." Formida stared into shifting shadows that was his skyline. The spy continued. "The reports point to the lords of the houses of the third, Ghom of gluttony; the fourth, Mammon of greed; and the ninth, Glabrezu of treachery, and the first terrace of the first circle, Egyn of Materials, who is also the instigator and spearhead of the rebellion. Our spies report that offers have been made to the second circle, ruled by Asmodeus of the lustful, to reign as acting supervisor until one among the kings could be chosen new ruler of Hell."

Formida nodded, handing the report back. "See this gets into the hands of Alastor. The fallen one is with them, and he will decide when best to strike." The spy bowed and exited, leaving Formida to his thoughts. *This is almost as dire as when Lucifer declined bowing down to the clay that was Adam. Well, Egyn, you overplayed your hand, and it is time you learned about the fury that is Hell.*

House of Alastor (Seventh Circle, Violence)

Alastor and Samgina stood on his balcony, overlooking the training grounds as the warriors went about their routine. "Tell me, Samgina, what are your thoughts regarding this renovation the Supervisor has undertaken?" Alastor asked.

Samgina's gazed stayed fixed on the fiery sky of Alastor's domain. "I have known Lucifer to branch off from the Chairman in only one incident, that which, of course, created this state we call Hell. I do not know Lucifer to make such a massive decision without the Chairman's blessing or acceptance." Samgina paused while Alastor patiently waited for Samgina to continue. A moment passed before Samgina, whose gazed had shifted from the horizon down to the training field, commented, "You undoubtedly have the finest warriors in all the realms, Alastor."

Alastor turned to Samgina, warning him. "Keep procrastinating, old comrade, and I might have to grace you with another smile," Alastor lightly threatened.

"The Supervisor forbid!" Samgina jokingly replied. "In answer to your question, I swore my fealty to Lucifer and Hell. It was we who first formed Hell and all its domains. What he decides, we shall do. Regarding Hell's expansion, I suspect *the Chairman* directed the Supervisor on this quest," Samgina earnestly shared.

Alastor snorted. "To what end? Did the Chairman not realize the trouble he would foment with such a demand?"

Samgina turned to face his comrade. "I would think the Chairman knew full well the repercussions behind such a directive and is more likely than not taking care of two imminent problems with one stroke," Samgina responded insightfully.

Alastor grunted. "I prefer direct combat compared to this backstabbing."

Samgina slapped his comrade on the back. "I agree it would be simpler if we could settle everything by force of arms."

Alastor nodded. "Shall we prepare the troops then?"

Gazing back to the blood red sky, Samgina hoped what he was doing was best for the realm of Hell. "It would appear that this is a good time to strike at our enemy as he seems disorganized. Let's begin by sending your troops to neutralize the threat of Nazarick the Wrathful as he is the most powerful of the foes. We will then send Formida's shock troops to disorient Glabrezu, keeping him chasing shadow troops in the ninth circle so he won't have a chance to engage us. I will convince Ghom of the gluttonous that he is fighting for the wrong side and that I would accept his fealty to me if he joined us in battle."

Alastor interrupted. "And why would Ghom do that? I'm sure the usurper has promised him ample reward for his allegiance," he said doubtfully.

Samgina nodded in agreement. "Of that there is no doubt."

Alastor continued. "Then my question stands. Why should he change sides?" he asked again, doubt deepening.

Samgina leaned against the bannister. "His nature," Samgina answered simply.

Alastor showed signs of frustration. "Forgive us as we are not all master tacticians, mighty Samgina," Alastor snapped testily.

"It is simple. Ghom is of the gluttonous, and the thing he is most gluttonous for is his existence. I am going to prove to him his existence would be assured if he sided with me," Samgina clarified.

"And how do you propose to do that?" Alastor insisted.

Samgina gave a wicked grin of his own. "By telling him that this is a purge designed by Lucifer himself to rid the kingdom of potential trouble in the new Hell."

Alastor looked shocked. "When were you going to tell me we had the Supervisor's support? When did he tell you this? Is he bringing many legions?" Alastor rambled, almost gleeful for the overwhelming firepower.

Samgina's smile deepened. "We don't, he didn't, and no," he replied.

A look of confusion settled on Alastor's face. "Samgina, what are you going on about?" It took a moment of Samgina basking in silence before understanding dawned on Alastor. "You're going to lie?" he asked, flabbergasted.

Samgina nodded. "Of course, I'm going to lie," he proclaimed.

Alastor looked uncomfortable. "I'm not sure I'm liking the notion of giving Lucifer a reason to be upset with us," he expressed vehemently.

Samgina smiled again. "I'm sorry. What would you expect from a demon in Hell?"

Alastor slowly smiled. "Do you think you can pull it off?" he asked slyly.

Samgina's smile deepened. "Most assuredly."

House of Ghom (Third Circle, Gluttony)

The sprawled province of Sloven, a terrace of the circle of gluttony, was crawling with the damned feeding on the feces of diseased carcasses. It was rank with the smell of decay. What saved the capital city from the stench was the infernal winds that spilled from the second circle of lust. The circle is chaired by the powerful demon king Ghom. Sitting on the throne of many layered skins and cushions, comfort and languishing was the order of the day for him. He used it as both temptation and punishment to have his will done. Beside him sat the great beast Cerebus, the three-headed beast that was the embodiment of greed, as when he fed, it seemed he was insatiable. It was rich as it bordered the realms of lust (second circle) and greed (fourth circle), two sins that mortals seemed to indulge more readily. Although as of late, Alastor (violence) had been getting its fill as the mortal world had exploded in population, so had its level of violence. Ghom's capital city of Plethora reflected its riches in the form of damned mortals slaving to build cities of bones and sinew lashed by tendons, supported by muscles, with eyes as windows and silently screaming mouths as doorways. The privileged of the other realms came here to indulge in the vices of the unnatural. The easy access to the second and fourth circles made it the idle spot for intense debauchery.

Ghom's slobbish assistant lazily strode into the vast throne room of Ghom. Portraits of all manners of lewd and decadent behavior decorated the walls. The best and worst of the three circles adorned the king's chambers. "What is it, Glut?" Ghom demanded.

Glut barely nodded, being so lazy, and dutifully reported, "Your Grossness, an emissary has arrived and requests an audience."

Ghom stared at his assistant. "And that concerns me how?" Ghom asked tiredly.

Glut shuffled in place. "I'm not sure how it concerns you, Your Grossness, but the one requesting leaves us with the notion that he is not to be denied."

This caught Ghom's attention because although his assistant Glut was a lazy pig of a demon, he had impeccable intuition, and to make such an impression on one such as he was worthy of attention. After a moment, the king decided, "Send him in then. And, Glut . . ."

Glut stopped hearing the unspoken demand for attention. "Your Majesty?" he asked, fully attentive.

"See to it proper security is set."

Ghom did not achieve or maintain his status through carelessness and was an old hand at the game. The position was initially held by Beelzebub, who seeded the position as unworthy of his former status (the god Beal). The position was a barren one as most ancient beings didn't have the resources to divulge in gluttony. Ghom, a lesser demon at the time, petitioned Lucifer for the office. After a few half-hearted skirmishes with competing demons, Ghom emerged victorious and not only took office but took an active role in petitioning the Dark Palace for unheard-of proposals. His first being the advancement of the Copper and Iron Age civilizations. It was the common belief and shared discontent that mankind should suffer as demons suffered and that their existence should be of utter misery. Ghom successfully argued that mankind would turn to the Creator more for relief from the sufferance; however, if humankind were given an abundance, they would soon abandon their Creator, who preached humility and shared wealth and common acceptance as opposed for the penchant of abundance and the birth of a new demon—privilege. This new demon would rekindle greed and desire and foment treachery in order to keep what they possessed. Ghom won the petition easily as all he predicted bore fruit.

The petitioner entered the lavish chambers and stopped in front of Ghom's throne. Dressed in a long robe and hood, the petitioner stood before the King of Gluttony. Ghom looked upon the hooded figure. "You stand before a king! What rudeness do you display?" Ghom demanded.

"The kind that was assured to get your complete attention," the petitioner responded, stripping away his hood.

Ghom drew in a deep breath. "Samgina!" Ghom almost yelped.

"Ghom!" Samgina replied, feigning surprise.

Ghom calmed himself. Besides, he was in the heart of his kingdom and concluded if he wasn't safe here . . .

Samgina smiled a small smile. He wished for the king to see his disdain. "You will not be safe, dread king," Samgina said, seeming to finish Ghom's thought. Ghom went over his intelligence report mentally, trying to remember if there was anything about Samgina having powers of telepathy. Samgina raised his hand for attention. "I come to you with these words, King of Plethora. Do not let your city fall to destruction. The usurper called Egyn has convinced many of the demonic houses to join him in a rebellion against the Supervisor, the master of Hell itself, His Infernal Majesty Lucifer—the very one that showed you favor by allowing you access to a throne. I do as I always have done to support him. I am one of the three that stood against the Chairman and fought against Micheal before we were cast down, Lucifer and myself on the torso of Perdition the Mighty. Now I hear that kings have sided against my lord whose full support I carry with me into battle. Know this, King of Plethora, if you side against me or His Majesty, you will beg for the relief of Hell and it will be denied you. Your comrades shall know suffering as no mortal can ever know."

Ghom shook his staff at Samgina, interrupting him. "Is the purpose of your visit to frighten me with threats?" Ghom nearly shouted.

Samgina shook his head. "No, King Ghom. I offer you the opportunity to not answer the call to arms when the rebels pit themselves against my banner, for under it shall be terrifying things. I bring with me wisdom, wrath, and shadows. Already the House of

Nazarick is being intercepted as we speak. I have put into motion the demise of the rebellion. Decide now," Samgina demanded.

Ghom looked upon the dreaded master of mystery. Samgina held the secrets of both Heaven and Hell, and Ghom was realizing that this mighty fallen one could have all of Hell had he so desired and that he, contrary to his demonic nature, still had a fragment of the light of Heaven in him. Not getting to his position by being a fool, Ghom conceded. "It shall be as you say, mighty Samgina. Upon the blowing of the horns of war, the House of Ghom shall not respond and will go further to pledge our allegiance to the House of Lucifer as we always have," Ghom said solemnly.

Samgina bowed. "As you say, King Ghom. Your word shall be your bond, and I'm sure His Majesty the Supervisor shall look upon you with favor in the new Hell."

Ghom held up his hand to stall Samgina's exit. "Mighty Samgina, what of the reports stating that many kingdoms shall fall under the thrall of others in the new master builder's designs?" Ghom asked.

Samgina's smile grew. "Worry not, Your Majesty, for the rebels shall suffer greatly and the royal, those that rebel, those that have their kingdoms only through Lucifer's will, shall find their kingdoms taken from them and divided among the loyal."

Ghom made as if to ask another question but caught the look in Samgina's eye and bowed. "As you say, Lord Samgina."

Samgina bowed his head in acknowledgment. "Your Majesty, it has been too long since we have feasted together," Samgina said in the manner of Plethora.

The king's bow deepened in acknowledgment of the courtesy extended. Ghom walked to his balcony to watch Samgina. Enthralled by one of the fallen, he remembered the mortal European Renaissance, a time that Europe celebrated as a lifting from the Black Death that had ravished a substantial portion of the civilized world. Samgina looked up, drawing the king's eyes to follow and beheld a legend.

"Majesty, is that Elan of the flame?" Glut whispered.

Ghom jumped, startled, then angry at being snuck up on by someone who had no hellish validation for being so stealthy. "Glut, what have I told you about slithering about like a worm!" King Ghom shouted.

Glut bowed. "Forgive me, Your Majesty, but I called you several times, and your gaze was transfixed outside, so I joined you and held the magnificent dragon," Glut explained.

King Ghom grudgingly admitted. "He is magnificent, is he not? Did you know he was said to have been born of the residual of Micheal's lightning and Lucifer's fire?" Ghom whispered.

Glut shook his head. "I had not, Sire. Is their concern for us with the fallen's visit?" Glut inquired.

Ghom considered a moment. "There was no visit, Glut," Ghom said with finality.

Glut nodded in understanding. "Will Your Majesty be taking his usual feasting?"

Ghom rubbed his hands excitedly. "Yes, by all means, let's leave this talk of battle from our roof and do as we've been dictated to do."

Glut looked off the terrace at the receding back of Samgina and Elan and realized his king had brokered a deal that would keep the circle of the gluttonous out of the upcoming war and garner favor with the avenging demon Samgina, true marquis of Materials, a prince of Hell, and one of the three directly cast from Heaven by the seraphim Micheal.

The Conspirators

The demon lords Asmodeus, Mammon, Egyn, and Nazarick gathered in a stone tower off the banks of the Phlegethon, near the domain of Alastor.

"Why did we pick this spot to meet?" Egyn asked in concern.

Asmodeus waved away the concern. "Alastor is not clever and would not think to look in his backyard for a potential enemy."

Mammon stood to speak. "I want to know where Ghom is," he inquired suspiciously.

Nazarick spat, "I tried to tell you that demon has no heart for this! He is a coward and can be depended upon only to—"

"Only to what?" Ghom asked, entering the chamber.

Shuffling behind him, his assistant Glut spoke, "It sounds as if they expected you to flee, my lord."

Ghom nodded in agreement. "It does sound that way, doesn't it?"

Asmodeus stood. "My ignoble brothers, for us to doubt one another now is folly. We have all seen what the new architect has planned for our kingdoms. Do any of you agree with this new arrangement he has devised?" Everyone shook their heads in negation. "So," Asmodeus continued, "what are we going to do about it?" Ghom shuffled to a stone bench, Glut came up slowly behind him and placed a plush cushion on the bench before Ghom seated himself. Nazarick closed his eyes in disgust. "So what did you have in mind Asmodeus"? Ghom sighed.

Mammon stood pointing out the imp in the room. "The first thing too remember is that we are not only going against the will of Lucifer, but he has Samgina taking up his cause even though Lucifer stood aside and did nothing when Egyn usurped his position."

Egyn stood angrily. "Who are you to cast dispersions on my method of acquiring my office?" he demanded.

"You misunderstand, Prince Egyn. I was not casting dispersions. After all, is this not Hell, and are we not demon lords? Speaking of feelings as if we were softhearted, heavenly entities sickens me. This is why I agreed to lend my support to this cause. We have become weak-willed sycophants, and I personally am tired of it and want to return Hell to the state of terror it once held dear," Mammon complained bitterly.

"I hear that the rumors of Lucifer has throwing his support behind the fallen Samgina is true". Ghom stated quietly. The demon lords looked at one another, concerned.

"Where have you heard this?" Mammon demanded.

"I have my sources," Ghom responded.

"That is ridiculous. Samgina would not fight for one who abandoned him," Mammon complained.

Ghom insulted Mammon with a smile. "I find it somewhat contradictory that one who is to gain from the new design to be so against it," he hissed.

Mammon looked furious. "You dare!" Mammon challenged.

"I do," Ghom answered quietly. "We have all seen the copy of the designs. This architect ridiculed the work of Mulciber and has claimed gluttony and greed as overlapping and thinks it should be assigned to your realm, Asmodeus," Ghom accurately stated.

"Which I reject!" Mammon The king of greed declared.

"As do I," Asmodeus King of lust declared. "I have more than enough to do without the burden of the gluttonous and greedy!"

"Well then", Ghom spoke in his slurred manner. "Perhaps we should begin to plan an attack as our opponents will no doubt prove to be formidable." They all nodded in agreement. "Very well," Asmodeus began, "I propose that Nazarick face the hordes of the heretics as they have expressed support for the toppled marquis upon Egyn's bid for the position of marquis of Materials and—"

"One second," Ghom intervened. "My understanding is that we would all agree before rendering assignments."

Asmodeus taloned hand slammed the table. "Are we a debate club? Decisions need to be made now, Ghom, not when everyone is comfortable with assignments!" he shouted.

No one noticed a shadow detach itself and exit the tower. The shadow agent swiftly reported back to his lord Formida of the meeting.

CHAPTER

12

From: Formida, Lord of Shadows
To: Samgina, One of Three

My lord,

Your predictions have proven accurate. The assumed parties have gathered at the suspected location, thinking to mislead us of their purpose. My agent has given a full account as to the intended parties' objectives. Within is a complete layout regarding time and Troop movements. We await your instructions.

Samgina read Formida's note and growled. Alastor looked up from sharpening his sword. "Helpful news?" he asked curiously.

Samgina looked at his comrade. "Apparently, King Ghom is either extremely clever or very stupid," Samgina observed.

Alastor stood, stretched his ridiculously muscled legs, and said, "Probably a little of both. What's the letter say?" Alastor inquired.

Samgina opened the letter. "Well, it appears those we thought a part of the rebellion is actually the heart of it."

"What! Those idiots are openly backing Egyn?" Alastor asked disbelievingly.

Samgina nodded. "So it would seem. They spoke of dividing the spoils of our houses and consolidating our kingdoms," Samgina summarized.

Alastor peered toward the horizon intently. "We should strike," he whispered.

Samgina stood beside him. "To do so at this time would give the appearance of us being the aggressors, and while we love mayhem, it would be very disturbing to the Supervisor's plan. And his piece is not yet ready for the board," Samgina said confidently.

Alastor turned to look at Samgina fully. "Is this nothing more than a game to you?" he asked disapprovingly.

Samgina turned to face his comrade. "The most serious of games, Alastor. I save my anger for battle. It allows me to see clearly," Samgina said coldly, giving Alastor, the king of the seventh circle of violence in Hell, a flicker of fear for this dread fallen angel, this one of three founders of Hell.

Alastor bowed his head. "What would you have us do?" the king asked.

Samgina pondered a moment. "I think you have a point in attacking, but we should do so subtly, as before but a bit intensified," Samgina responded.

Alastor clapped his hands together. "Excellent! What did you have in mind?" Samgina divulged his plans, making Alastor bear his terrifying grin again. "Another day in paradise," he growled.

Hell's Rebels—Chorozon, King of the Sixth Circle (Heresy)

The Lord of Heresy himself was overseeing his staff's preparations for the arrival of the fallen and his comrades. Never in Hell's history had his circle been so close to be a part of crowning the new ruler of Hell. (It came close once during what the mortals called World War II. The lies, misinformation, and propaganda were accomplishing wickedly delightful results until the brutish mortals reverted to savage violence and dropped atomic weapons.) But now they were invited to partake in what was sure to be recorded in the annals of hellish history.

"Slave, why has the feast not been displayed?" the king shouted at his assistant.

Anzu bowed and clapped his hands. Half a dozen damned souls appeared, filling plates with fresh meat. (Flesh of the vilest sinners were masterfully seasoned with the tears of widows and orphans with just a touch of the expelled excrement of the unjustly murdered.) Amid the servants giving orders to them was Joseph Goebbels, the Nazi prime minister of propaganda. Like his fallen comrade the master architect Karl Bischoff, Goebbels utilized the brutal tactics he honed in his mortality with the Nazi regime and succeeded to the position of the assistant to the deputy, and while it was a fact that Herr Bischoff's position was much more prestigious than Herr Goebbels, the master architect was civil enough not to treat him too badly. After all, this was Hell. Goebbels understood.

The table was set; the blood was poured. The king clapped his hands, and Anzu ushered everyone from the feasting room. Chorozon passed the neatly aligned tables and rows of straight-backed chairs. Looking around, he noticed and hastily pointed to a portrait of two of the three upon Perdition plunging into the depths of infinity. Anzu straightened the portrait as it was askance. "Well?" Chorozon simply inquired.

Anzu bowed. "My liege, your banquet awaits its guests," Anzu responded formally, an odd thing about the House of Heretics. The king demanded formality and a hellish form of decorum. Anzu bowed. "Your Majesty, your guests have arrived. If I may?"

Chorozon waved his hand dismissively, and Anzu transported to Castle Paganus's entryway, where the three kings and the Fallen awaited. "Your Majesties, our apologies for any delay. Will you join His Majesty King Chorozon in his banquet chambers," the deputy assistant of the House of Heretics requested.

Samgina frowned (a compliment). "If you would lead the way, ignoble Anzu," Samgina grunted.

A deep frown creased Anzu's face. The demon lords were escorted by Anzu as he led them to the feasting chambers. Portraits of some of Chorozon's conquests decorated the walls, from the first mislead, which was brought about by Sameal convincing Eve to eat from the tree of knowledge, to popes who permitted and demanded the execution of the Cather's to the present. A portrait of Joseph Goebbels hung their as well as he misled millions of Germans into hate-filled frenzies against innocent Gypsies and Jews, leading to their summary executions. The demon lords were greeted by Chorozon as they entered the chambers. "My lords," he greeted, "please, before we are about our business, I ask that you sit and have your fill of the finest Hell has to offer."

Alastor plopped his massive frame before the king could finish and ravenously tore into the fresh meat and drank deeply from the goblets of blood. "My lord," Alastor grunted between slurps of blood, "this meat is delightful!"

Chorozon frowned. "How am I not surprised that the king of violence would not enjoy the fresh meats seasoned as it is?" Chorozon quipped.

Alastor raised a goblet in salute. "In that you are correct, my lord. This meat is to die for." The kings laughed. The other kings joined Alastor at the table and partook of the meal. After which, they retired to Chorozon's chamber of contemplation.

"My lords, I welcome you to Castle Paganus, and we curse the meal we shared. I shall now request Samgina to address this ignoble body as to his plans to depose the insolent kings of chaos. My lord." King Chorozon bowed.

Samgina stood. "Gratitude to His Inglorious Majesty Chorozon for hosting our gathering. I will keep this short as we all have serious duties to attend. As you all know, the upstart Prince Egyn of the House of Elios made a bid for my seat. Instead of deposing him, I abdicated, so I could find the source of his newly found support system. I knew with Lucifer's new directive, he would not be focused on the recent events occurring in his domain. I have found Egyn's support system and was shocked to learn that at its head sat Asmodeus, with Astaroth, the treasurer, sitting in the shadows. That said, we shall leave Astaroth to Lucifer's judgment, but the others, well, I've devised a plan of attack that should have us sitting here again, drinking in victory. My plan is as follows. Alastor will take his hoard and contain Nazarick the Wrathful at the fifth circle, not allowing him to link with his allies. I cannot stress enough how vital this is as Nazarick would be the most troublesome when it comes to direct battle."

Alastor stood, banging his goblet. "You have chosen well, Lord Samgina. I will be pleased to show this miscreant the errors of his ways," Alastor boasted.

Samgina nodded in approval. "We shall, Before we strike, send the shadowed agents of the House of Formida to infiltrate and, through misinformation, confound the directives of both Malbolge of the eighth circle and Glabrezu, the warden of the ninth circle, effectively keeping Satan out of the battle. As for our host King Chorozon and myself, we shall confront the so-called marquis Prince Egyn as well as Asmodeus, who seeks the kingship of Hell, and his lackey Mammon.

The signal for attack is when you hear the beasts of Hell roar the trip chord," Samgina finished.

"A question," Formida posed. "How will we be able to hear you in the eighth and ninth circle if you're at the second circle of Asmodeus? With the roar of the infernal hurricane and, remember, the bull king stands guarding that domain?"

Samgina frowned deeply. "Cerebus is a part of the fiefdom of Ghom, Regent of the gluttonous, and he was assured a part of the feast that shall come from deposing the upstarts," Samgina clarified.

Formida continued, "But, my lord, was it not reported that Ghom attended the war council of Hell's traitors?"

Samgina nodded in agreement. "So he did, my lord, and he would have been a fool not to, because then the usurpers would have known he was not alongside their cause. And because his military strength is not formidable, they would have isolated him, and his kingdom would have been the first to fall."

Alastor seemed unconvinced. "And you know this how exactly?" he asked.

"Ghom is anything but stupid, and I convinced him that anything else besides aiding us would, in fact, be incredibly stupid."

Alastor sat down, not fully convinced, but what was a good war without risk? "Are we in agreement then?" Alastor asked.

The kings stood, raising their goblets. "To Hell, to war!" they saluted.

Heaven

The seraphim Archangel Metatron, also referred to as the Voice of God, tried to fathom the unfathomable as he soared closer to the Essence. In his mind, he heard a chuckle. "Yes, Father, millennia pass, and we continue in folly," Metatron capitulated.

The chuckle softened. "My child, it is what compels you to understand the depths of the nature of things," the Alpha's voice said in instruction.

Metatron stopped moving as moving had no real meaning in this notion of eternity. "My lord, is it our intention to allow Hell to fall into disarray?" Metatron asked. An amorphous, pulsating energy mass appeared before the archangel; he bowed his head in obeisance.

The energy mass slowly shifted to form an elderly mortal. Metatron dropped to his knees.

The Alpha smiled. "Please get up," he asked softly. Metatron rose in an elderly form, a smile creasing his angelically beautiful face. "Tell me, child, if I had appeared in regal form, you would have . . . ?" the Alpha trailed off.

Metatron allowed his chest to swell as he postured. "Then I would have made myself as grand as my Creator made me, for I mirror him in all things," Metatron responded authoritatively.

"And this?" the Alpha asked, passing a wizened hand over his elderly form.

"When my lord appears humbly to me, so then shall I, too, be that which he made me," the angel responded.

The elderly manifestation of the Creator smiled beatifically. "You are wise, my dear child, and to answer the question of Hell, I think things will work out just fine," he answered, smiling into the cosmos, watching, transfixed. (Only Micheal, Lucifer, and Gabriel had had the grace to be beside the Creator when he worked.) "You see, my child." The crackled voice of a matronly woman rang out. Metatron forced himself not to look and kept his eyes on the event unfolding in what now became a section in the cosmos. The Creator smiled, revealing broken and cracked teeth. Metatron turned to face his Maker and fought the compulsion to laugh. "What do you find so funny?" the Creator asked, poking Metatron with a bony finger.

Retreating a step on what was now a veranda overlooking a formation of "star cradles," Metatron, in return, chuckled. "I am blessed that you love me as you do." A field of energy pulsated varied colors where the elderly woman had stood.

"Bless you, Metatron. Have no concerns for Hell, for it will do as Hell does, and the one most worthy shall rule it. Instead, turn your concerns to the mortals whose desire for power shall turn upon them and visit upon themselves a dire corruption that would consume them."

Metatron stood before the archangels. It took a moment to reorient himself.

"What did he say?" Micheal asked quickly.

Metatron slowly gazed from Micheal to Gabriel then to Phanuel. Metatron smiled. "In short, mind your own business."

The Grand Summoning
Bischoff—the Unveiling

Bischoff stood on the left-hand side of the stage behind the blood-red curtains overlooking the Dark Palace's auditorium. The seats were quickly filling with the rank and file of Hell. Princes of all the kingdoms with their archdukes, bishops, and servants amassed in this accursed chamber to hear the decree the Supervisor would be imposing. While all received the general notice, this was the detailed summary of the plan, and it affected every denizen of the infernal regions. There were pockets of outraged demons that such power should be given a damned soul, but of course, no one stood and outright opposed the directive of the Supervisor, who, by the way, was oddly absent.

Astaroth stepped up to the podium, holding his hands up to quiet the murmuring that filled the air. "My demonic kin, royals, and nobles, we have assembled here today in order to waylay any suspicions, rumors, and doubts as to the events we have been currently undergoing." The huge crowd grunted, moaned, and hooted in unison. Again, Astaroth raised his hand, and the clamor subsided. "Now we have brought before you one that has been chosen by the Supervisor, Lucifer, himself to explain the process of renovation. As explained by His Majesty, these dictates are irrefutable, unarguable, incontestable, definitive, and conclusive. Noncompliance shall be met as an open attempt of rebellion and will be noted as treasonous, and the offending party or parties shall be relegated, ostracized, and exiled upon pain of spiritual punishment or obliteration. So ordered by His Majesty Lucifer, King of Hell," Astaroth concluded, looking out into the now silent room. "Now without further delay, I present to you the one the Infernal has dubbed master architect of new Hell, Master Builder Karl Bischoff."

Karl, who had been standing on the wings, wondered if Astaroth just intentionally set him up to fail and fail miserably. How does one reconcile the surrendering of kingdoms to an angry crowd? Karl straightened, remembering many of his old comrades were out there in attendance. This was his opportunity to show all how powerful the Nazi party actually was to fashion Hell itself. Karl strode out confidently, which a few demons noticed. He marched up and stopped before Astaroth and nodded in salute. "I thank you, Lord Treasurer,"

Karl asserted arrogantly and somewhat dismissively. While this angered Astaroth, who revealed his annoyance by narrowing his eyes, there were those in the demonic ranks who were not overly fond of the royal treasurer and others who outright despised him, and among these, Bischoff got a more willing audience.

Karl stepped to the microphone. "My fellow denizens of most inglorious Hell." A roar resounded in the depths of the massive auditorium. "I was cursed by the master with the most terrible of tasks. It was perhaps my punishment, my torture, my private Hell. This is Hell. Unlike most mortals, they are coddled and bunched together in these pits to witness one another's suffering. Not me. No, I am relegated a Hell that shall not see redemption because my Hell affects Hell itself!"

A murmuring of misunderstandings filled the room. Bischoff waited for it to subside and spoke forcefully, "But this is Hell, right? We do what we must because only we can bear the shifts in eternity that need bearing. The powers that be does not ask Heaven to bear any universal attrition and entropy. Only the might of Hell may do so. However, I took it upon myself to design a plan that would provide the most long-term benefits that we so richly deserve for accepting such a monumental task. For this, for the inglorious manner of our suffering, will you but give me your ear and consideration?" Bischoff concluded his opening introduction.

News traveled at the speed of the Dark Palace's propaganda machine, which was diabolically fast, throughout the kingdoms of Hell. Karl stepped back a moment and sipped from his goblet, as was customary. The chatter from the spectators was loud and presumptuous. It was mostly judgment on his speech and delivery. (Remembering, of course, this was Hell, and who here wasn't under some form of judgment?) The arguments ranged from the audacity of Lucifer to issue such a threat-filled address to the filthy damned soul he recruited, presumably without input from the royal council or even his own advisors. While others found the seemingly direct approach of the master builder forthright and worthy of an unbiased hearing. The contrary nature was to be expected, and Bischoff realized he could not have hoped for better. Bischoff opened his folder and withdrew documents that bore the infernal royal seal.

Those in front, glancing at the documents, ceased their random conversations and gave their full attention to the damned soul who was going to dictate the immediate future of Hell. The unrest was palatable. Tension filled the surroundings as if it were an intangible spirit. Karl broke the seal to the envelope that held his plans for a new Hell. This was the moment he both anticipated and dreaded. Failure meant. *You are in Hell, you fool!* he admonished himself. He slowly withdrew the drawing plans, set them aside, and also withdrew documents emblazoned with the Dark Palace seal. He slowly and deliberately tapped the papers on the table as if to align them, but it was actually done to find out if Karl could hear the sound receding far into the chambers, informing him that everyone was indeed hanging onto his words.

"My fellow denizens, please allow me to preface this by saying some of the directives here may be distressing to some. Understand I did everything I could possibly do to minimize any inconvenience. There is also the abolishment of repetition for the sake of efficiency in the form of the merging of sins into similar categories." Bischoff paused to see if there was any reaction. Uncharacteristically, the demons remained quiet. This admit-tingly made Karl apprehensive, but he continued. "It is my sad duty to report the following. The third circle currently being ruled by Ghom as Beelzebub's regent as well as the fourth, which is run by Mammon, that is, the circle of greed and gluttony, shall fall under the domain and new rule of the second circle, the circle of lust ruled by Asmodeus. The princedom will be assigned to Mammon. Ghom shall assume the position of viceroy." A murmur ran through the assembly.

Ghom rose from his position, who was quickly followed by Glut, who chased him, beckoning, "Your Majesty, please wait."

Bischoff watched them leave. "The sixth circle, heresy, under King Chorozon, and the eighth, fraud, ruled by Malbolge, shall be combined with the ninth, treachery, ruled by Satan with Glabrezu as his regent. The hellhound Cerebus of the third circle shall be reassigned to the Avenue of the Damned as guardian and chief tormentor, formally known as the Road to Perdition. Cerebus will patrol its broad expanse, harassing the damned as they make their way to the Gates of Hell. Minos shall be stationed there to assign the damned their eternal suffering. The Acheron, the River of Woe, will continue to be the source of the Rivers Phlegethon [River of Fire] and Styx [River of Hate]. The River Lethe, however, shall be rerouted to the second circle, falling under the dominion of Asmodeus. The nine circles shall be renovated into nine squares. Each square shall be accountable to the new office of infernal affairs, whose staff shall be elected by the newly appointed kings. All these directives have been approved for immediate confirmation by the King of Hell, and all redress shall be addressed by His Majesty the Supervisor and King of Hell Lucifer. This concludes this briefing." Karl exited the auditorium rapidly as it exploded into discussion by some, debate by others, and downright argumentative shouting by the disenfranchised.

Mammon could be heard growling. "Who does this piece of dragon shit think he is coming here and saying I'm redundant?"

Malbolge sat rock still, appearing to fume in anger. He silently rose and exited. A shadow slunk out to report the event to his king.

House of Shadows

The shadow knelt before Formida and reported the events of the summoning. Formida looked at his spy. "Go now to the domain of Alastor and report all to him. I'm sure Lord Samgina will want to move quickly." The shadow departed. Formida rose from his throne and summoned his commander. "Prepare our troops for deployment. I want you to take a detachment to stifle Mammon. I will take a company and descend to the ninth circle to keep Glabrezu and Satan occupied," the king ordered.

"But, my lord, how shall we know when to strike?"

The king frowned. "Samgina promised a signal unheard of in Hell's existence, so be ready," he responded.

The commander nodded. "As you command, my lord."

CHAPTER

13

Kingdom of Malbolge (Eighth Circle, Fraud)

Malbolge paced his throne room. "Who does this monkey think he is telling a lord of Hell what he will and will not be doing? What he shall and shall not rule?" Malbolge raged. Malcoda sat back wisely and stayed silent. "Arrogant pond scum! And Lucifer, what was he thinking allowing such a thing? Malcoda!" Malbolge yelled for the aide who sat so quietly Malbolge hadn't noticed him.

"Yes, my lord?" Malcoda said softly.

The demon king fixed his aide with a hard stare. "See to it we get an immediate audience with Asmodeus," Malbolge demanded.

Malcoda bowed. "As you wish, my lord."

Malbolge waved his hand in dismissal. Malcoda hastily went to do his master's bidding. "We shall see if Asmodeus truly has the will or is posturing to see who will capitulate from fear. Treachery is my domain, and if it is a spell he casts, then I shall break it," Malbolge hissed.

Ghom (Second Circle)

The second circle was in a barely controlled frenzy. The king was grunting at his panting aide. "We have been betrayed, Glut!" the king ranted. "We are a pillar of Hell. How is it feasible that they would strip us of our wealth and status?" Ghom demanded of his demonic assistant.

"My lord, it is His Majesty's dictate. Dare we disobey it? the cost of rebellion, and besides . . ." Glut trailed off.

Ghom peered at Glut. "Samgina," he whispered.

Glut nodded vigorously. "Let us not forget, my lord, to do so would invite disaster. I dread his fury above all others."

Ghom stared at Glut and stomped his foot. "Yes, of course, we shall enforce our agreement with the fallen."

Glut frowned deeply. "Shall I prepare, my lord?"

Glom's face grew stern. "First, summon Cerebus to me," Ghom ordered. Ghom grabbed a quill and sat at his desk to compose a letter.

> From: Ghom, Regent of the Third Circle
> To: Samgina, the Fallen
>
> Dread Lord,
>
> All has come to pass as you predicted. I find myself in a tenuous position as the current dictates of the Dark Palace basically strips me of power and status. This is most unseemly as the proper execution of gluttony helped propel Hell to its current prosperity. To be now ejected from favor seems inconsistent with the policy of His Majesty, casting doubt on the authenticity of today's proclamations. That said, allow me to reconfirm my commitment to the cause.
>
> Yours in the passion of Hell,
> Ghom

Alastor (Seventh Circle)

Alastor and Samgina sat together by the River Phlegethon, the River of Fire. Alastor found the heat soothing. "The battle is upon us, mighty Samgina," Alastor commented aimlessly.

Samgina grunted assent. "It is, cruel King, the traitors have made themselves known."

Alastor stared into the blaze of the river. "What of Ghom? Will he stand beside us, or has his gluttonous nature directed his decision?"

Samgina considered the question. "According to Formida's spies that attended the summoning, Ghom himself was displaced," Samgina pointed out.

Alastor looked at Samgina. "Yes, it also stated that Mammon has been displaced, that both Mammon and Ghom are to surrender their authority to Asmodeus," Alastor rejoined disbelievingly.

Samgina nodded affirmatively. "While that may be so, Mammon is extremely untrustworthy. I see him challenging Asmodeus's authority, but if Asmodeus remains steadfast, then I do not see Mammon attempting his own coup. No, indeed, I see him waiting on the sidelines until Lucifer makes his presence known, for His Majesty is the unknown factor in all this."

Alastor nodded in agreement, stood, looked at Samgina who remained seated, and extended a hand to assist Samgina to his feet. Samgina looked up into the red-tinted eyes of Alastor then at his huge hands and quipped, "You know, I'd be unable to fight if you rip my arm out of its socket." Samgina scoffed.

Alastor barked, "You will not lull me into placenscy with your flattery, fallen one. I am aware who I address." Alastor, king of the circle of violence, responded with fear in his voice.

Samgina frowned. Still looking at the huge extended hand, Samgina responded, "That being said, Alastor, King of Violence, you have allied yourself to me and offer your sword against those that seek to displace that which was, is, and ever shall be the rightful ruler, sanctified by the Chairman, who we call Lucifer, Morning Star."

Alastor locked eyes with Samgina. "Let all those that would rise against us suffer the fury that is Hell!" Alastor exclaimed vehemently.

Samgina clasped Alastor's hand. "It be so," Samgina cursed, yanking himself to his feet.

Asmodeus (Second Circle)

Asmodeus sat on his ruby-and-pearl-inlaid throne. "Tell us, Murmur, did the royal houses seem disposed to obeying the Luciferian dictates?" Asmodeus hissed at his chief administrator, Murmur the Calabite.

The scribe mumbled his reply. "My lord, of the four kings dispossessed, I would give thought to look to Malbolge with caution. He could be a worthy ally yet is treasonous in nature."

Asmodeus considered for a moment. "Explain yourself, Murmur," Asmodeus ordered.

Murmur reflected a moment, gazing at the decorative throne; its inlay was lovers entwined in sexual ecstasy. Murmur looked into the alabaster eyes of his master. "My lord, Malbolge will come to assess your resolve." Murmur paused, keeping his eyes on Asmodeus.

"Go on," Asmodeus barked impatiently.

Murmur continued. "Your distaste for, shall we say encounters of exertion, will probably lead Malbolge to the assumption that you are posturing, thus striking at his vanity, for treachery is his domain, and if anyone assumes the mantle of supervisor and supreme ruler of Hell, it should be him, at least under those circumstances," Murmur concluded.

Asmodeus considered what his aide said and slapped the arm of his throne. "Let him come. He shall bear witness to our resolve," the would-be ruler of Hell huffed. A minion slunk into the presence of the two and whispered in Murmur's ear. Asmodeus waited for the minion to leave and asked, "What is it?"

Murmur looked from the retreating back of the servant back to his king. "My lord, Malbolge has arrived and seeks an audience with you," Murmur reported.

Asmodeus frowned. "Very well. Show him in," the king ordered. Murmur bowed and turned to do as ordered when Asmodeus called to him. "Murmur, a moment. After showing Malbolge in, I require you to go to the first region and inform Egyn that his presence is required here," Asmodeus barked.

Murmur bowed. "As you command," Murmur complied.

"Also, tell him to be prepared. If my conversation solicits the support of Malbolge, we shall go to war immediately!" Murmur bowed again and exited the throne room. A moment later, Malbolge entered, escorted by a minion.

The minion spoke aloud, "Your Majesty, may I present Lord Malbolge, King of Fraud, Lord of the Eighth Circle." The minion bowed out of the infernal majesties' presence.

Asmodeus stared at Malbolge. "How goes it, brother?" Asmodeus said in greeting.

Malbolge stared at the King of Lust. "Do you truly seek the rulership of all Hell, Asmodeus, or do you speak in falsehoods, awaiting unchallenged capitulation?"

Asmodeus frowned. "My resolve is absolute, King of Fraud. After all, treachery is your bailiwick. I shall defend the validity of my claim as I sent into motion the things required for this event to occur," Asmodeus responded fiercely.

Malbolge grunted, "So you say, lustful one, but remember, I have seen you make such claims before and retreat at the first sign of strong opposition."

Asmodeus fixed his alabaster eyes on Malbolge. "I assure you, King of Fraud, that I will ascend to the throne and have not only a powerful alliance supporting me but also have the words of Lucifer himself in his dictates!"

Malbolge glared at Asmodeus. "There was nothing in His Majesty's dictates that speak of Asmodeus, King of Hell!" Malbolge spat. "So wherefore did you come by the delusion that you could occupy the unholy seat?" Malbolge asked contemptuously.

Asmodeus leaned forward on his throne. "You are the one that deals in fraudulence, Malbolge. It is not . . ." Asmodeus paused, listening intently.

Malbolge caught the look of curiosity on Asmodeus's face. "What is it?" Malbolge asked, concern in his voice. Asmodeus looked at Malbolge with disbelief, impossibly glazing his white eyes. Malbolge glared, feeling a creeping sense of dread. "What in the deepest pits is happening, Asmodeus?"

"Do you hear that?" the King of Lust asked again.

Malbolge paced back and forth angrily, paused, and listened. "I don't hear anythi—" The King of Fraud paused and slowly realized what Asmodeus was referring to. "The winds," Malbolge whispered.

Asmodeus nodded. "The winds," he confirmed.

"But how?" Malbolge asked, concern deepening.

An unexpected roar shook the pillars unto the very foundation of Hell as both kings looked at each other, awestruck, as they heard the elemental dragon Elan, Minos the Minotaur, and Cerberus in unison sing the tritone, the devil's interval or the chord of evil. The chord would never be sung in Hell because it was very unlikely the trio needed to sing it would ever ally, yet for reasons that escaped Asmodeus's reckoning, they had, and that chord summoned great armies of Hell into motion. An explosion followed the silencing of the chord, snapping both Asmodeus and Malbolge into awareness.

"We're under attack!" Asmodeus screamed.

"Who would dare!" Malbolge shouted.

"Is that something you wish to consider now?" Asmodeus shouted in return.

Murmur burst into the throne room. "My lord, the River Lethe has been breached. Many of our troops were camped there in preparation for a sojourn into the deeper circles in order to lay siege to Alastor's kingdom," Murmur reported.

"What of Alastor? Where is he now?" Asmodeus asked after a moment of thought. As if on cue, a minion brought in a report and handed it to Murmur, who looked at it. "Well?" Asmodeus demanded impatiently.

"My lord," Murmur whispered, "it is reported that Alastor marches on the very capital itself. That he and his giants have Nazarick besieged!" Asmodeus shook with rage.

"I must get word to Malcoda!" Malbolge shouted.

Asmodeus shouted at Murmur, "Take what is left of our legions, gather Ghom's legions—"

"Stop, you fool!" Malbolge yelled at Asmodeus.

"What did you call me?" a furious Asmodeus challenged.

"You're not thinking," Malbolge declared. "The chord. The chord came from the direction of the third circle. Minos was part of the trio, Cerebus is of the that, and it sounded as if Samgina's elemental dragon Elan was the third. My guess is that Ghom was infuriated at the dismantling of his kingdom and agreed with . . ." Malbolge paused, considering. He smiled a disturbing grin at the audacity of the planned events now occurring, but if any one could do it, Samgina, this reticent master of Hell, could. "We must summon Egyn to us," Malbolge declared, snapping out of his reverie.

Asmodeus snorted derisively. "Why do we require his presence?"

Malbolge glared. "Do not forget that the renovation was the pretext for us going to war. This battle that is about to take place falls on the plot of Egyn's usurpation of the marquis of Materials' position."

Call to Judgment

With the silencing of the great tritone, Alastor rose in his saddle. The enormous scaled war hell rhino shifted beneath him with a desire to crush things underfoot. Alastor gave the command to charge. "For Hell! For Lucifer!" Forty-five legions of demons marched against the capital of Hell and the city of Dis. The first troops deployed were the stone hounds and the harpies. The shriek of the harpies kept the furies off-balance, neutralizing their effectiveness, and the stone hounds negated the power of Medusa, who, alongside the furies, stood as captain of the gates. The ravaging hordes of Alastor clashed against Nazarick's demons. As the battle became pitched, Nazarick unleashed his furious horde to turn the tide, holding in reserve his vengeful horde, knowing his opponent well. Seeing the releasing of the reinforcements, Alastor sent in his legion of psychopaths to even the battlefield. Once more, the battle became pitched. Knowing he had more in reserve, Nazarick deployed his wrathful to outflank the enemy only to run into Alastor's giants who had anticipated the move. The field became quickly soaked with demons' gore.

Nazarick dipped into his surprise. "This should teach the arrogant fool!" Newly enlisted into the demon ranks from damned soul status rose Achilles, sworn servant and general of the legions of Asmodeus. With Achilles rose Diomedes, captain to Achilles and commander of the elite demon force of the Mymidons, Achilles's earthly warriors that were rapists of men, women, and children during their conquest. Under loan from Asmodeus, the general stood tall before Nazarick.

"Your orders, great King?" Achilles probed.

Nazarick pondered, looking out at the battlefield, trying to assess where Achilles would be most useful. "Outflank the giants, and it will collapse their protected side, giving the wrathful time to regroup and overwhelm the giants." Achilles thumped fist to chest plate in salute and went to join the battle.

Nowhere

Lucifer poised at the edge of existence, gazing between the nothing and the everything. A soft, warm light joined him. "Knew I'd find you here," a voice said gently.

"What do you want, Metatron?" Lucifer responded tartly, annoyed by the intrusion.

Metatron's astral form coalesced beside Lucifer. "I guess that question could be aimed right back at you, but for now, let's stick to the more salient question," Metatron proposed.

"And that would be?" Lucifer countered factitiously.

Metatron faced Lucifer. "You do realize that Hell is currently going to Hell as multiple factions have risen in your absence with means to usurp your throne!" Metatron voiced pointedly.

Lucifer continued to stare out at the creation's cauldron. "I remember when I was first summoned here," Lucifer reminisced, "I stood in awe of everything, and as the Creator imparted his divine plans to me, I trembled at the enormity of it. Now I am in dread. All seems to hang on the slimmest of threads . . ." Lucifer trailed off.

Metatron took a moment before responding. "It would be disingenuous to say I understand you, Lucifer, and you may scoff at my relatively naive perspective, but the Chairman brought forth the perfect Supervisor. And despite apparent differences, we of the seraphim class support your administration. Do not lose faith, Morning Star!" Metatron professed strongly. Before Lucifer could respond, the one of two sounds that could pierce the dimensions touched them. "This is why I came," Metatron informed Lucifer as the warmth of the Creators blessing came over them.

Lucifer frowned, turned to Metatron, and smiled angelically. "My hopes are realized and come to fruition," Lucifer claimed gleefully.

Metatron looked upon him. "So it was your intention all along to get Samgina to fight your battle?" Metatron asked, somewhat perturbed.

"No, no, no, not at all," Lucifer denied. "I knew there would be a rebellious response to the Chairman's directive, so I watched as parties took sides. What the objectives of those sides were and my greatest concern was that my brother Samgina might have been a part of it. After seeing the attack on his seat of power by the nefarious Egyn and the traitor Amayon, I knew my brother would return masterfully, leaving me to carry out the Chairman's directives unburdened by the trivialities of civil war."

Metatron pondered the information. "Devious, I admit, but won't Samgina be resentful for being used in such a fashion?" Metatron queried.

"Not when I explain in full, he won't. My brother considers himself the Defender of Hell, a title I will officially entitle him with. He is the balance between the Pride, the Tempter, and the Accuser. And now if you'll excuse me, I must prepare my mount for our grand entrance into the fray," Lucifer pled.

Metatron bowed. "As you will, Lord of Retribution."

Lucifer smiled. "I rather like that," he said, fading out.

Second Circle (Kingdom of Asmodeus, Lust)

Egyn was ushered into the throne room by Amayon under protest. "How dare you hurry me along as if I'm some sort of beast! Remove your hands from my person!" Egyn demanded.

Amayon had tried to assist this reckless, pompous demon prince whose only qualifying factors were that he was of Hell's ignoble families and that he was fortunate enough to be in the right place at the right time, and it was proving to be more of a burden than anything else. Asmodeus's plan was simple. Wait for Lucifer's departure, which Asmodeus knew was going to occur once Lucifer began the renovation in earnest. If the obnoxious little prince could follow through on the plan and remove Samgina from his seat, then use the simple, prideful prince demon Egyn as a figurehead for the rebellious faction (with which the House of Malbolge was of great assistance spreading the rumors that Hell was being handed over to a mortal and the kingdoms were being torn asunder). Lies based on a truth tore Hell in half, and now Amayon, who had placed his stakes alongside Egyn, stood beside his master, hoping the fool would not speak out of turn.

Asmodeus stared at Egyn. "Explain yourself!" Asmodeus demanded vehemently.

Egyn looked at Asmodeus with a bored expression. "What need have I to explain myself to you, Asmodeus?" Egyn asked, sarcasm dripping.

Asmodeus glared at Egyn, livid. "Prince Egyn, are you not a descendant of the House of Elios?" Asmodeus asked needlessly.

Egyn looked up from his talons arrogantly as if bored. "I am," he answered simply.

Asmodeus leaned forward from his throne where he sat. "Well, you know that your house is in service to mine, so if you would please—" Asmodeus was silenced by the roar of a dreaded foe. "Elan," Asmodeus whispered.

Egyn stared, eyes wide with fright. He looked fearfully to Amayon, who showed resignation on his face. "Amayon, what is it?" the frightened puppet asked.

"Our doom," Amayon whispered.

Asmodeus yelled from his throne, "To arms! The enemy is upon us!"

CHAPTER

14

Rise of the Fallen

With the sounding of the tritone sung by the three beast kings of Hell, all hellish activities ceased. The infernal hurricane that tortured the lustful, the never-ending winds, ceased. The damned were not being punished, the power of the rivers receded, and the Lethe no longer stole thoughts of hope, love, or joy. The Phlegethon no longer seared souls or the Acheron bring woe; even Styx and Charon were stilled as the newly named Avenue of the Damned was closed as the great kings of Hell engaged in battle. The mightiest and forefather to the dragon race descended from the pitch skies of Hell into the capital city of the second circle. Ridden by the powerful Samgina, the two proceeded their armies, landing in the center of the square of the Palace of Lechery, where Asmodeus held court. Samgina sat on Elan and waited. The yard quickly filled with the combined troops of Asmodeus, who were supported by Malbolge's terror demons (especially despicable-looking with protruding fangs and talons dripping with venom). The kings Asmodeus and Malbolge, accompanied by Prince Egyn, stepped out onto a stone balcony overlooking the parade ground.

"Samgina!" Asmodeus shouted in greeting. "What brings you to my palace of pleasure? Do you seek respite from your weary travels in oblivion's halls since your denouncement?" Asmodeus said factitiously. Samgina sat silent on Elan's back. "Come now, mighty one, surely you've not come to sit mute?" Asmodeus taunted.

Samgina pointed at Egyn and Amayon, who stood beside him. "I would have words with the traitor and the usurper," Samgina grumbled. Asmodeus looked at the prince and his assistant. "Give them to me, renounce your petty bid for the throne, and I will spare you," Samgina offered with the threat of violence in his tone.

Asmodeus chuckled. "You have courage, Samgina. I'll give you that," Asmodeus offered.

"You give me nothing, Asmodeus. Even if you gave me your contempt, it would mean as little to me as you do," Samgina growled menacingly.

Asmodeus appeared offended. "What have I done to earn such contempt from you? You come to my realm with armed soldiers without invitation. What gives you the right to enter my kingdom with such disrespect?" Asmodeus demanded.

Samgina smiled. "You did, King of the Lascivious,"

Asmodeus shook his head in denial. "I did no such thing," Asmodeus insisted.

"You did!" Samgina insisted. "You did when you decided to draft the fool prince beside you into being the face of a rebellion that has no just cause other than your lust for power," Samgina said pointedly.

Asmodeus leaned on the balcony. "Lies! You come to spread lies! Did Chorozon feed you these lies?" Asmodeus asked defensively.

Samgina fixed Asmodeus with a stare. "Give me what I demand or suffer," he warned. Asmodeus quickly considered his situation. His great general had currently been reassigned, the belief being that if their grab for power met with resistance, keeping Dis under their control would lend validity to their claim. He looked sideways at Malbolge, who lifted his eyebrows in a quiet response Asmodeus found difficult to interpret. Samgina saw the look flash in Malbolge's eyes and addressed him. "Great King of Treachery, you know I speak with substance. Had Asmodeus's lust for power not blinded him, he would not have chosen this fool dressed as a prince who does shame to his inglorious bloodline, the grand House of Elios,"

Egyn stepped forward, hearing the insult, furiously stating, "Renegade, cast out! Do you think you have cause to speak to your superiors in such a fashion? I should have your tongue cut out and fed to the hellhounds for such insolence."

Samgina grinned widely, revealing pearly white teeth with canines that looked needle sharp. "Do you mean these hounds?" He let out a piercing whistle, and on a nearby hill behind the palace walls appeared the three-headed form of Cerebus, who stopped and howled.

A moment later, the surrounding hills were filled with hellhounds as they obeyed their master's commands. The kings watched as the hills filled with snarling hounds. "Consider this, Malbolge," Samgina began. "You wisely take your warriors back to your kingdom, and Lucifer will deal with you in his own way or face obliteration. Before you answer, consider again, Who stopped the infernal hurricane of lust? Who brought the three beast kings together to bring forth the tritone? Who now sits before you on the back of the most powerful beast king in all creation with legions of hellhounds and their king to battle you? What is your answer?" Samgina demanded.

Ninth Circle

Glabrezu ran around in a very undignified manner as he vainly tried to keep order. As regent of the circle, it was his responsibility to not only maintain the punishments of the traitor souls condemned here but was also tasked with keeping Satan restrained and dormant (under Lucifer's edict) while simultaneously yet secretly looking for any viable opportunity to break the chains of Prometheus and the red string of fate that bound him (Satan's command before bound) so that Satan would rise as master of Hell, something a few of the royal houses would have preferred. Glabrezu reported to his master, "Lord, all goes according to your desire. The houses are stirred against your calmness and wish for the days of old when we terrified mankind and laid waste his dreams. They tire of residing in the shadows in which your calmness has resigned them."

Satan stirred imperceptibly. "Prepare then. Prepare my courts to receive me and let us lay waste to what the Morning Star has achieved since he has seen fit to exile me, his better side, in the chambers of his guilt!" Satan exclaimed furiously. "Have you approached Sameal with my offer or Envy with my enticements?" Satan moaned in agony.

"My lord, neither are to be found. Our agents searched but have found nothing."

"Prepare . . . prepare," Satan whispered. What Satan failed to realize or chose not to realize was that his own domain was under nefarious attack by Formida and his house of shadow demons, who were disrupting every function imaginable, except for the torture of Satan, which continued unabated, which confused Glabrezu, who had no idea he was under a covert attack meant to disrupt and immobilize and not destroy (which would have been flagrant and noticeable). The mission given to the shadow king was to subvert yet remain undetected, a job well suited to the King of Nightmares. Formida kept the regent in enough shadow with disinformation and small acts of sabotage, incapacitating Glabrezu from fulfilling his undeclared duties (the release of Satan).

Fifth Circle—Battle for Dis

Giants swept demons aside, clubbing others with huge cudgels. Achilles prepared his Myrmidons. The southern gates of Dis were thrown open, and he charged out into the battlefield, striking down his enemies as they appeared. He faced Balor, the one-eyed giant, on the back of his horse Hrungir.

"Give yourself to me, little man!" Balor shouted.

Achilles raised his sword and charged with his Myrmidons behind him, screaming maniacally. Swords rang, demons screeched, and giants roared as Achilles and his damned souls joined the fray.

Second Circle—the Choice

Samgina waited for Malbolge's response. Malbolge looked at Asmodeus. "Well?" Malbolge asked.

Asmodeus looked at Malbolge with concern. "Well what?" Asmodeus asked in return.

Malbolge motioned to Samgina. "May we have a moment?" he asked courteously.

"Take two," Samgina approved magnanimously.

Egyn protested loudly as even his shallowness saw things turning out badly for him. "Silence!" Malbolge ordered.

Flustered, Egyn screamed. "How dare you treat me as a pawn! Do you think for a moment this treatment will be tolerated once the royal consul hears of it?" Egyn claimed, sounding offended. Malbolge and Asmodeus led Egyn, who was closely followed by Amayon, back into the throne room. Egyn spun to face the Kings of Lust and Treachery.

"What are you doing? Were you seriously ready to hand me over to that savage?" Egyn complained, fear tinging his words.

Malbolge looked at Asmodeus. Sauntering to his throne, he considered the situation. "We should transport Amayon his assistant to Nazarick, in the fifth circle and request the immediate return of Achilles and his Myrmidon to deal with the fallen," Asmodeus suggested. Malbolge nodded, agreeing. They motioned for Amayon to stand in the center of the room, doing as ordered by the kings. With a gesture Amayon was instantly transported to the reception area of Nazarick.

Dis was under attack. Alastor had the capital under siege. Amayon appeared amid the screams of violence and mayhem as only the King of Violence knew how to bring it. Looking for King Nazarick, Amayon stumbled into Carreau, Nazarick's general, who was shouting orders, directing various factions, trying to make a cohesive unit of the many demon tribes. "Where is the king?" Amayon shouted over the noise.

Carreau looked as if just noticing him. "Who the hell are you, and why the hell are you asking me questions instead of fighting?" the general shouted back.

"I am Amayon, council to Egyn, Marquis of Materials, sent to give a message to the king," Amayon reported.

Carreau shook his head. "I have no idea where His Majesty is, although it's possible that he is facing Alastor and his giants."

Amayon ducked as a projectile flew close by. Nodding understanding, Amayon went in search of the King of Wrath. Nazarick (whose fury often overcame his common sense) was leading a contingent of the carnage division positioned just outside the gate, trying to cut a swath through Alastor's center. Amayon cautiously stepped past the king's flanking guards and approached the mighty King of Wrath. Amayon looked upon the king in awe. He was captivated by Nazarick's infernal majesty. If only Egyn was just a shadow of this inglorious king, he could have served with distinction, but because of the prince's character flaws, which revealed his idiocy, Amayon found himself in a very precarious position.

"Your Majesty!" Amayon shouted over the din. Nazarick's eyes of blazing fire turned to stare at the fool who dared disturb his pleasantry. Amayon tried to push down the terror he felt. "Forgive the intrusion, Your Majesty. I come with a request from King Asmodeus regarding the possible transfer of Achilles and his Myrmidon as Samgina has appeared at his gate and a battle has ensued." Nazarick's eyes actually dimmed in intensity at the absurdity of the request. He impatiently gestured to the battlefield, waved his hand, and transported Amayon back to Asmodeus's throne room.

Denial

Amayon found himself standing in the center of the throne room. Egyn was the first to address him. "Well? Where is Achilles?" he shouted.

"Nazarick is under siege by Alastor of the seventh circle. He has brought Balor, the one-eyed king and his Formorians," Amayon reported.

Egyn began to tremble. "What are we to do?" he nearly shrieked. "We have the beast kings against us as well as the traitorous acts of Ghom. How can we . . ." Egyn trailed off. "What of Glabrezu and Satan? Surely with them we can still be victorious," Egyn pointed out.

Amayon shook his head. "I'm sorry, my lord, but the last report we received was that both Satan and Glabrezu were being successfully engaged and occupied by the House of Shadows," Amayon stated quietly.

Egyn voiced his fear, "The House of Nightmares have joined with Samgina's cause? What are we to do?"

Asmodeus looked toward Egyn. "Perhaps it is time you lived up to your family name, demon prince of the House of Elios," Asmodeus said challengingly. Egyn looked terrified. Amayon got a small frown he quickly hid.

"Are you fucking insane? Do you know how much fury he has toward me?" Egyn asked selfishly, forgetting or dismissing that Amayon would also face Samgina's wrath.

Malbolge tilted his head, pointing out the obvious, "Well, you did usurp his kingdom."

Egyn spat, "You coaxed us to do that! You had a grand plan that would elevate all our houses, and Hell, through Asmodeus, would have a new ruler!"

Asmodeus frowned at Egyn. "I told you that any implementation of our plan would depend on you successfully ousting Samgina," he said pointedly.

Egyn began to shake, seeing where this was leading. "I did!" Egyn screamed. "I did depose him!"

Asmodeus shook his head. "No, he unseated himself. You did not recognize the why of what he did and, considering yourself successful, came to us with wondrous praise for yourself, never realizing that you were being led into a trap."

Egyn began pacing. "Neither did anyone else!" Egyn screamed.

Malbolge frowned. "While that may be so, none of our necks were on the line had you failed, which you did miserably, and now you have one of the mightiest demons on the back of a beast king of Hell who is allied with the other beast kings, and they are calling your name, Egyn."

Egyn was horrified that his plans had gone so badly. He turned to Amayon, who had already began walking to the balcony. "Where are you going?" Egyn shouted at him.

Amayon turned. "I go before my former lord and shall accept what I am due," he said with finality, spun, and walked through the curtains.

"Well, I'll be damned before I go out there and depend on that savage's mercy!" Egyn shouted at Amayon's back.

Malbolge smiled at Egyn. "Sad to see your assistant has more courage than you do."

Egyn shook his head. "Don't confuse stupidity with courage." Egyn scoffed.

Malbolge barked back, "I never do!"

Amayon approached and walked through the doorway of the balcony, stepping out. The first thing Amayon noticed was the dull lackluster sky of Asmodeus's domain. The second and more shocking was the stilling of the infernal hurricane. (As told by others, the winds were a torment for the insatiable nature of lust.) Amayon walked to the short stone wall that served as a barrier and looked over to see the great dragon Elan, and sitting atop was his former master, Samgina.

"Amayon," Samgina called upon seeing him. "Have you lost weight? You look thinner, not well at all," Samgina said with what Amayon believed to be contempt.

Amayon bowed his head. "I have wronged thee and stand before you humbled and prepared for punishment," he said in a near whisper. Samgina smiled. Amayon bowed his head lower at the insult.

"Amayon, Amayon, why when you had it all, you wanted more?" Amayon raised his head as if to answer, saw the look in Samgina's eyes, and realized the statement was rhetorical. "I do not care that you admit your faults. That is an act with the presumption of forthcoming forgiveness. This is Hell. We don't do forgiveness here. Fortunately for you, that other thing you were prepared for, we do in abundance, so I may grant you punishment befitting your acts. But let us not minimize, shall we?"

A terrified Amayon squeaked. "Minimize, my lord?" he asked in dread.

"Yes, minion, minimize!" Samgina responded acidly. Amayon's demeanor stooped as he heard the first of the judgments against him. His first punishment was demotion from a demon earl of Materials to a mere minion, servant to any demon that demand service from him no matter what the service entailed. "You dared insult me by calling your acts of betrayal as wronging me?"

Amayon saw his pride get in the way. "But I served you well, and you rarely graced me with your presence or guidance," Amayon demanded.

Samgina frowned, amused by what he heard. "Amayon, have you been to Heaven lately? They're really big on all the things you just mentioned, like guidance, forgiveness, and a pat on the ass when you're a good soul. Unfortunate for you, we don't do that here. No, here we punish, and you, my traitorous former earl, shall visit and keep company your comrade in arms in the ninth circle. Give my regards to Glabrezu, say hello to Satan, and bring something warm to wear." The last thing heard from Amayon was a bone-chilling scream as Samgina transported him to the frozen lake of Cocytus.

Egyn turned a terrified face to Asmodeus and Malbolge. "He has the power of transporting? Why didn't we know that?" he asked with trembling voice.

"Samgina is a founder of Hell! Didn't you stop to think this, among other powers, was his to wield?" Malbolge asked as if speaking to a child.

"Of course not! Why should have I known?" he asked stupidly.

Asmodeus shook his head in resignation. "Because, fool, it is standard practice in any war to know the capabilities of your enemy before engaging them in combat."

Egyn began nervously pacing. "He was never my enemy, only a means to an end. When I heard Amayon complaining about his incompetent master, I thought . . ."

Malbolge let out a long sigh. "By the Supervisor's fangs, how can you be a part of an ignoble house and not know the history of Hell?" he complained.

Egyn crossed his arms. "Do you know how boring those lectures are? I would sneak off and come here to sample the fine wares Asmodeus has running around."

Asmodeus stared at Egyn. "This is the price for such privilege. I think you should go out and face the situation you created because you don't want the rest of your clan to know that you shirked your final duty and left them to suffer a fallen one's wrath because you were afraid to." Egyn stood horrified, knowing he was losing the support of his colleagues.

CHAPTER

15

Last Call

C arreau joined Achilles and his army as they prepared to charge into the fray. "General, we have to aid the king! He is at the main gate holding back the hordes of Alastor," Carreau commanded.

Achilles looked at the regent of Dis. "My lord, do you not see Balor the Giant and his horde descending upon us? Let us smash through them first, then we can aid the king."

Carreau looked up to see the giants running down the hill toward them. "Give the order, Achilles!" he commanded. The great warrior of the Trojan wars lifted his hand and signaled the charge.

Second Circle—the Master Arrives

Egyn walked to the doorway of the balcony. He could hear Samgina berating Amayon and heard the demotion and the punishment bestowed upon him. Trying to hide the terror that was building inside of him, Egyn glanced back at his supposed allies and grunted. "Watch now the courage of the House of Elios," he stated before parting the curtains and stepping out unto the balcony. Samgina, who still sat on Elan's back, watched the idiot Egyn walk out onto the balcony and noted the look of dread battle with the demon's pride.

"You were cruel to our former servant, Samgina." Egyn observed aloud. Samgina remained silent. "Nothing to say, fallen one?" Again, Samgina said nothing. "You do realize it was not personal when I caused your abdication." Samgina only glared at him. "You need to understand that there was a lot bubbling under the surface, and you seemed to refuse to address it. When our former servant, Amayon, came with a proposal to remove an ineffective member of the royal caste that cares not for his position or Hell itself, it seemed the only thing to do was force your abdication. Please understand, I'm not trying to excuse what I did. I'm only explaining to you, because as a member of the royal bloodline, you would not, could not accept such a servant, so I believed you would understand my deeds." A quiet Samgina stared at a babbling Egyn. "Well?" Egyn complained. "Aren't you going to say something?"

Samgina smiled. "Are you done?" he asked quietly.

"Am I done? What do you mean am I done? Of course not! I am a prince of Hell, and my duty is to . . ."

Samgina whispered in Elan's ear, "Burn."

White hot flame shot out of Elan's gaping maw, bathing Egyn in flames. The former prince of Hell and marquis of Materials let out a high-pitched scream, "AHHHHH!" The agony-filled scream sent shivers down Malbolge's and Asmodeus's spine. The audacity of Samgina to incinerate a member of a noble house was unprecedented. Such an act was unconscionable. The kings felt a fear they had not experienced in a millennium.

Malbolge turned to Asmodeus. "What kind of fighting force remains?" he asked, furious at his own fear.

Asmodeus looked to Murmur, who reported, "My lord, of our seventy-two legions, fifty remain. The rest are under the influence of the Lethe and have no memory as to their tasks."

Malbolge looked at Malcoda, who promptly reported, "My lord, we still have our full contingent of forty-five legions."

Malbolge nodded at Asmodeus. "Let us release our forces upon the upstart."

Asmodeus nodded to Murmur, who ran out to the balcony and shouted, "To arms! To arms!"

Elan reared up ready to blast the regent when the tri-chord sounded again. This time, the composer of the theme sang it. Appearing on the back of the beast, Lucifer, armed with his trident of dominance, roared. "By my order as master of Hell, I command for all conflict to cease immediately!" he bellowed loudly. Battle in all the circles ceased. Much to the dismay of the rebelling kings, the combatants, seeing Lucifer with his trident and mounted on his beast, fell to their knees in supplication. The Morning Star's bellow could be heard throughout the entirety of Hell. "Let the kings of all the domains come before me. Let none be absent from my court. You have been tested and found wanton."

Samgina dismounted Elan and knelt before his master. Lucifer gazed at him. "Most loyal servant of Hell, your seat, authority, and privilege is returned to you, and your judgment shall be as decreed. Eygyn" You shall know the horrors of betrayal."

The rebels trembled in terror. To the ninth circle, Egyn was cast to serve a furious Satan and suffer constant punishment under the watch of Glabrezu, who himself was punished, but to a lesser extent, as he was not directly involved with the rebellion. Satan thrashed in fury for the denied opportunity to escape the chains and red string that bound him.

"Let all those summoned attend me when called upon. My loyal marquis of Materials will honor me with his presence forthwith." Lucifer then vanished. The beast was placed back in the bottomless pit as Lucifer returned to the Dark Palace.

Violence Silenced

The battle for Dis ceased immediately when Lucifer's command for cessation rang throughout Hell. Achilles and his Myrmidon reluctantly stopped fighting. Balor and his giants lowered their weapons. Harpies and wyverns stopped their dive-bombing Nazarick's troops. Nazarick himself had difficulty with the cease-fire and stomped back and forth, glaring at the powerful Alastor, wishing to do battle with him. Alastor returned the stare with equal vehemence. The air was filled with the stench of war; it also was becoming crowded with scavenger birds. Hell's version of the avian species ranged from flesh-eating bird/bat mutants, dung-eating vultures, and omnivorous razor-clawed pigeons. (These are the beasts that ate of the flesh of mortals that walked in the Creator's light.) The beasts dive-bombed the many scraps and whole pieces of demon flesh that played scattered about the field.

Upon seeing the disgusting yet necessary beasts swooping in, Nazarick glared at Alastor and shouted, "You've managed to escape my wrath again, Alastor! Lucifer must be guarding you, mindless one!" He taunted.

Alastor gripped the hilt of his sword tighter. "So screamed the petulant upon his retreat. had not His Majesty called a halt to this skirmish, your dung-eating pets would be feasting on your carcass even now. Say what you will, but we could always meet when all has been settled and Hell is again itself," Alastor retorted.

Nazarick glared. "So we shall, mindless one," he spat.

Alastor glared back. "May Lucifer hasten the time, obstinate dog." Nazarick spun his griffin, who eyed Alastor hungrily, toward his capital.

Judgment—Pandemonium, Dis

Bells rang in celebration of the return of its ruler. The denizens of the City of Pandemonium lined the roads that led to the capital. Demons, picas, minions, and all sorts of denizenry ran about as the recently war-torn city returned to a semblance of normalcy. The pitch of the tormented returned to near frenzy as the recent cessation of punishments resumed in full measure. The blood red-tinted sky was free of attacking harpies, griffins, and wyverns. The minions were occupied, cleaning the streets of the many demon corpses from both Nazarick and Alastor's armies that littered the many roads. What the scavengers missed in their initial feeding was swept up and dumped in the Phlegethon to burn away. (of course the demons or damned souls could not die but if their hacked up bodies didn't reform fast enough they were scooped up as waste and punished further by the river of fire).

Lucifer sat on his throne of wood (from the tree of knowledge of good and evil), bones (from those sacrificed in the name of evil), and tongues (from those who spoke against the word of the Creator). This gruesome throne was graced by the awful form of Lucifer, who, in stark contrast, held his court.

Karl Bischoff, the master architect, stood at a table with the floor plans of the renovated Hell. He was explaining the design and the improvements that his design brought. "My lord, on the Road to Hell, now renamed the Avenue of the Damned, I have covered the floor with sin-sensitive saw-toothed thorns (allegedly from the crown of the crucified one) so as the condemned slowly make their way to the gates, the thorns shall pierce the skin of their bare feet in accordance to their sins.

Lucifer frowned. "Nice touch," he observed.

Bischoff tried not to swell with pride and noticed Lucifer peering at him. Stammering, he continued, "I assigned Cerebus to run up and down the avenue to harass the condemned with everything, from snarling at the less sinful to mauling the corrupt." Karl paused; it was quiet for a moment.

"Are you waiting for me to comment on everything you describe, Bischoff?" Lucifer queried.

Karl felt the terrible pressure of Lucifer's attention upon him. Trying not to shrink, he answered Lucifer, "No, my lord, I just wished to pause in case you wished to correct or dismiss an idea."

Lucifer sighed. "I will stop you if need be. Now go on," Lucifer commanded. Bischoff bowed.

Just then, Ibliss entered the throne room. "My lord." The assistant bowed.

"Yes, Ibliss, what is it?" Lucifer asked him.

"My lord, the rebel kings await your pleasure," Ibliss announced.

Lucifer nodded. "Allow them entry when Herr Bischoff leaves," Lucifer commanded. Ibliss bowed and exited the chamber. Lucifer turned back to his chief designer. "So you wish to move my pets around and displace some of the royal houses? You didn't think this would be met with resistance when you chose to remove Ghom from his seat of power and have him subject to Asmodeus?" Lucifer asked with a raised eyebrow.

Bischoff bowed his head. "My lord, I think the sin of gluttony and lust to be variants of one another and thought it wasteful to consider them separate entities," he stated confidently.

Lucifer shook his head. "That is because you think as a mortal. I assure you, if your perspective was from an immortal standpoint, you would see how they differ," Lucifer instructed.

Bischoff wisely tempered his reaction at the criticism. Bowing his head again, he responded, "It is as my lord says. My perspective is narrowed with mortal constraints. What would my lord have of me?" Karl asked, feeling somewhat deflated.

"Worry not, Master Builder, I like much of what you have done. Retire now while I attend to matters requiring my attention. I shall summon you, and we shall finalize the plan," Lucifer ordered.

Bischoff bowed. "Yes, Sire." Bischoff obeyed and exited the throne room.

Ibliss poked his head in the entryway, looking at Lucifer, who raised his hand as a signal. Ibliss nodded and returned a moment later with the royal party he had dubbed rebel kings. Ibliss escorted the royal group before Lucifer's throne. "My lord, I present the complaining party, King Asmodeus of the second circle, Lord of Lust, and his compatriots, Ghom, King of Gluttony [third circle]; Mammon, King of Greed [fourth circle]; Nazarick, King of Wrath, Satan's representative; Malbolge, King of Fraud [eighth circle]; and Glabrezu, King of Treachery [ninth circle], as well as Satan's warden, and finally, Egyn, former Marquis of Materials of the House of Elios, who was set aflame by Lord Samgina before being cast into the ninth circle for his betrayal." Ibliss gestured to the second party. "My lord, the party of the counter complaint is Samgina, Marquis of Materials, and his allies, Alastor, King of Violence [seventh circle]; Chorozon, King of Heretics [sixth circle]; and finally, Formida of the House of Shadows." Ibliss finished the long but traditional acknowledgments.

Lucifer considered the assemblage. "Lord Samgina," Lucifer acknowledged his comrade.

Samgina nodded. "My lord," Samgina replied simply.

"Brother, I must impose upon our relationship with the understanding that I would never forget one of the three that stood beside me in defiance against the high seat of the Chairman," Lucifer began.

Samgina interjected. "It has never been my intention to question your motives, Sire. Since we stood before the throne of power, my allegiance has always been to you," Samgina whispered with as much humility as his mighty persona could evince.

Lucifer frowned. "And for that reason, I am honored to have one such as you beside me," Lucifer stated in a rare complimentary moment. "I acknowledge that your loyalty and actions have provided me with the time and distraction I required to fulfill the directives of the Chairman." Lucifer's stare shifted from Samgina to the rebel kings who stood as a group. "Asmodeus, you scoundrel, how is it that after thousands of millennia, you have yet to master your own urges?" Lucifer asked rhetorically.

Asmodeus stepped forward boldly. "My lord, the vice that is lust is voracious and ever famished, never to be sated, so I . . ." Lucifer held his hand up for silence. Asmodeus trailed off into silence, watching Lucifer intently.

Lucifer stared at Asmodeus for a moment. "What the hell is wrong with you Asi?" Lucifer asked with disgust, surprise, and strangely enough, sadness mixed together. Asmodeus's will deflated, seeming to have abandoned him at that moment, hearing the name Lucifer called him when he was first recruited for his position as demon of lust. "Instead of damning you to a vulgar pit, I lifted you to a position that allowed you to eventually become king in your own domain, and you repay me with betrayal?" Lucifer, whose voice had started in disappointment, now built into a tempest as he roared at Asmodeus. "What say you to these charges of treason, King of Lust?"

Asmodeus fought not to fall on his face before the fury of the Morning Star. "My lord, nothing I say can abrogate my deeds. You were gone. No one knew where. A mortal from the depths rose and, with your seal in hand, began to tear Hell down around our ears and began to tell of a new Hell and how kings of old would have to surrender their seats of power and become subservient in other domains. I thought, how could this be? Nay, it was not. This clever little monkey found a way to force our lord from his seat, perhaps even banish him, and sought to gain control of Hell. So in defense, I gathered allies for the sake of Hell and thought to do battle for the Supervisor's position as I believed you to be gone," Asmodeus claimed proudly.

Lucifer tapped his lip as he sat back on his throne. "So let me see if I understand your claim. You raised an army, gathered those beside you, convinced them that what? I abdicated? Was supernaturally kidnapped or was indisposed?"

Asmodeus was silent for a moment. "My lord, my argument was simple," he answered simply.

Lucifer waited a moment. "Excellent! It should not be difficult to explain then," Lucifer quipped.

"My lord, we didn't know what to think. We knew only that you were gone with an edict from the Chairman, so we were not sure if the orders were for you to abdicate for some heavenly reason or a directive so distasteful to you that you simply left," Asmodeus said in explanation.

Lucifer looked to the other kings. "And you, Mammon, the same reason?" he asked. Mammon simply nodded in confirmation. After a moment of silence, Lucifer's attention focused on Malbolge. "And you, King Malbolge, what have you to say?" Lucifer prodded.

Malbolge locked eyes with him. "It is as Asmodeus claimed. We decided as the kings of Hell that the throne should not sit empty, so we agreed that Asmodeus should take up the seat."

"My seat!" Lucifer interrupted.

"Your seat," Malbolge agreed. "So that Hell would not be masterless and become chaotic."

Lucifer stood. "The rest of you agree with what has been said so far?" he inquired. The remaining kings nodded in agreement. "Minos," Lucifer called out from behind the throne. The great judge stepped out before the audience who bristled at his appearance.

Nazarick spat out, "My lord, we object!" He complained.

"So you speak for all in this?" Lucifer asked.

The kings nodded affirmatively. "He does," they answered in unity.

"So be it," Lucifer agreed. "Speak, King of Wrath," Lucifer said with a tone of hostility creeping forth."

Nazarick paused a moment as it occurred to him that he just placed the burden of judgment upon himself by agreeing to speak for all. "My lord, the judgment of Minos is unwarranted here. If you feel as if we acted beyond our position, then we beg judgment separate from the damned but rather consideration worthy of our positions," Nazarick begged.

Lucifer appeared to consider it for a moment. "Tell me first, King of Wrath, where was this consideration you speak of for me? Which one of you approached my regent Ibliss for information? Did any of you approach my comrade Samgina? No, you didn't, and why? Because from the moment I took leave to be about the Chairman's directive, you scandalous scum"—Lucifer pointed to the kings—"went about dividing Hell among yourselves, ousting my designer and calling to arms your legions to do battle with anyone that had loyalty to me!" Lucifer ended with a pitched voice.

Nazarick bowed his head. "It is as you say, my lord," the King of Wrath quietly admitted.

Lucifer looked up from the king. "Does anyone else wish to beg for forgiveness before Minos casts his judgment?"

Asmodeus stepped forward. "Lucifer, might you not be overreacting? After all, we are the royalty of Hell. Did you expect any less from us?" Asmodeus complained.

Malbolge, encouraged by Asmodeus's argument, stepped forward. "It is as King Asmodeus says. We did only as you yourself have done. When the Morning Star was absent during different parts of mortal history, the rule has gone from Sameal to Satan to you, Lucifer. The mighty Samgina himself is a member of the House of Sameal was once offered the position. Why than should we be punished for something you yourself had done when you went through your stages of awareness?"

Lucifer sat back on his throne and shot a hard look at Malbolge. "The answer to that does not aid your case in any way, deceiver. What I find interesting is that not one of you have addressed me properly, choosing instead to speak on familiar terms with me, which indicates to me no remorse. So seeing that you have no remorse for the revolt against your lord and master, I shall ask Minos to begin his judgment." The rebel kings bristled.

The huge bull king of judgments walked in front of the infernal throne. With Lucifer sitting on the now blazing throne, Minos pointed at the kings in front of him. "Nazarick," Minos declared, "shall no longer be titled King of Wrath. His seat shall be entrusted to Azazel. Demon of War, come forth!"

In a cloud of sulfuric smoke, Azazel, the demon who taught man the use of weaponry, appeared and knelt before the infernal throne. "My lord," he stated simply.

Minos looked down from his place. "You have been charged and elevated. Do you swear alliance?" Minos asked.

"I do swear allegiance to Lucifer Morning Star, as my rightful ruler and lord," Azazel replied fervently.

"Go then and ascend to your throne, and all hail the new king of wrath!" Minos declared with a voice that rang throughout Hell. The rebellious kings, facing their final defeat, knelt in homage.

Azazel rose with new power and authority. He looked to Lucifer, who nodded and gestured toward Nazarick, who, with the removal of his powers, seemed to have withered and shrunk to the size of a minion. Azazel strode toward Nazarick, who shrunk away from the ferocious newly made king. "Come, slave, and know the agony of betrayal!" Azazel demanded, reaching out and snatching the diminutive demon and disappearing in a cloud of smoke.

Minos's finger rose from its side and pointed at Malbolge. "For giving ear, counsel, and arms to dethrone your rightful ruler, you, Malbolge, are so judged with removal of your seat of power. Your kingship will be given to Dolo-Yama. Demon of Treachery, come forth!" Minos bellowed loudly. The demon appeared and gave his oath of fealty to Lucifer.

Malbolge stood defiant. "My throne is my own! I shall never surrender my crown or power!" he shouted wildly.

Lucifer appeared bored. "Really, Malbolge? Even in the end, you lack grace. You believe the powers are your own?" Lucifer mocked. He looked to the new king of treachery. "Be about your business, Your Majesty," Lucifer commanded.

'Yama smiled and bowed to Lucifer, spun on his heel, strode over, and snatched a feebly resisting Malbolge by his pointy ears, twisted them, and growled at Malbolge. "You will learn your rightful place or suffer, slave!" And with that, they vanished.

Minos's finger slowly moved to Mammon, who stared desperately, trying to figure a way out of his predicament. He raised his hand. "If I may?" he began. Lucifer raised his hand, and Minos paused. "Consider this, mighty Lucifer. Few have been here as long as I. Removing me from office at such a time might prove calamitous for you, as any new king would have tremendous difficulty appropriately assigning punishments because we both know the new breed of condemned souls have the powerful impetus of capitalism, compelling them in a fashion never known to mankind. With despotism or even monarchy, the peasants accepted their lot in life, but with capitalism, everyone is raised to believe they can become wealthy, so greed abounds, and the billions of new souls we are about to receive would be a burden even to one as experienced as myself," Mammon finished, confident he made a valid point as he watched Lucifer pause and lean back on his throne.

"That is a quandary," Lucifer admitted. Mammon fought the impulse to frown. "But if even you would have a difficult time, you still serve no purpose," Lucifer pondered aloud.

Mammon quickly interjected, not wanting his chance to vanish. "My lord, I did not say or mean to imply that the deed is insurmountable, only that through my vast experience and knowledge would the categorization of avarice be done in an efficient manner," Mammon urged with a hint of pride.

Lucifer again appeared to ponder. "And how would you do that? A feeling? A glint of the eye?" Lucifer queried.

Mammon confidently frowned. "I would sniff them out," he declared.

Lucifer snickered. "Come now, Mammon, you mean to tell me that you can actually smell greed?"

Mammon stood from the kneeling positions the kings took. "That is exactly what I mean. I can smell greed emit from a newborn and entice them during their life to the pits of Hell," Mammon bragged.

Lucifer considered this, and the remaining kings for the first time looked hopeful. "It is as Mammon says. This is going to be a difficult time for proper assignments, and we are grateful for his insights." Lucifer looked to Minos and nodded.

Mammon opened his mouth to complain. "My lord! Did you not hear? It would take . . ."

Lucifer raised his hand, and Mammon fell silent. "We heard and understood your punishment will serve Hell. That is your wish, is it not? To serve Hell?" Lucifer posed.

Mammon knew he was in trouble but could not fathom its meaning. Trapped by his own words, Mammon agreed, "Yes, Lord."

Lucifer nodded. "Very well. Please continue, Minos."

The terrible judge spoke, "We call forth Belphagor and raise him up." Belphagor, the demon that corrupted the souls of men of avarice, rose from the depths. Upon appearing before the throne, he dropped to his knees and swore fealty. Lucifer fixed his gaze upon the new king of greed.

"As pointed out by the rebel, your upcoming task shall be daunting, and though you whispered the dreams of wealth into the ears of mortals, knowing the total greed in a mortal's soul or recognizing the depths of that greed, so I shall render aid to you," Lucifer warned Belphagor.

Then turned to Minos, who declared, "Rise, Leopold of the Belgians, king, colonizer, and usurper of a nation's wealth." Leopold appeared trembling from his punishment to find himself before the ruler of Hell. He dropped to his knees.

Lucifer leaned forward. "Leopold, former king of the Belgians, are you prepared to leave your punishments in order to serve Hell?" Lucifer asked.

Leopold stood. "How may I be of service to Your Majesty?" he asked.

Lucifer frowned. "Follow all the dictates of Belphagor with your ultimate loyalty to me, and I shall elevate you," Lucifer declared. Leopold fell to his knees and made his oath. Lucifer looked at Minos, who in turn looked at a very frightened Mammon. "You were right in saying your expertise would have been useful, but you will continue to serve, and your power shall not be stricken." Mammon frowned deeply, misunderstanding Lucifer, who had turned to Minos, nodding.

"For your treachery against your lord, your crown and authority is removed and your power and form shall be diminished to the shape of a pig. Not a boar with tusks that might defend itself but a pig—a pig that shall suffer the compulsion to eat the feces of minions and picas. And the more you eat, the more powerful your sense to detect greed shall become and the desire for power," Minos declared in judgment. Mammon attempted to protest but could only squeal as the transformation occurred as Minos spoke it.

Lucifer looked toward Belphagor. "The pig of greed and Leopold are your assistants and servants. Use them well." Belphagor bowed, and the pig ran to his feet, snorting. With Leopold, Belphagor, and the pig disappearing in a cloud of smoke, Lucifer turned his attention to Glabrezu, who stared at the floor. "Have you nothing to say, guardian of the spiteful?" Lucifer asked.

"My lord, forgive me, but your dark self spoke of the old days of true evil, when we walked among mortals causing their fall," Glabrezu sputtered.

Lucifer looked at the warden of his rebellious nature and said softly, "I rose you up and gave you but one task, to guard and ensure the imprisonment of my radically rebellious nature. Instead, you allowed yourself to be seduced by a power that serves only itself in direct betrayal to the one who lifted you up." Glabrezu said nothing. Lucifer turned to Minos and nodded.

Minos pointed to Glabrezu. "For failure to fulfill your task, for the act of treason against your master, you are consigned to the ninth circle, stripped of rank and privilege. But because of your loyalty until this point, Lucifer is not unmindful of the difficulty of your task, so you shall be demoted to the rank of demon to serve under the demon/ warden Ahpuch, whom we now summon."

The air swirled as the demon appeared. Dropping to his knees before the throne, he rose, swelling with the power of his newly acquired kingship. He bowed to Lucifer, nodded to Minos, and quipped, "Worry not, Sire, I have a worthy punishment for the ungrateful." He snatched Glabrezu and vanished.

Lucifer looked upon the remaining rebels. Asmodeus stood defiant. "Well, what do you think?" Lucifer asked Asmodeus. "Was my wrath justified?" Lucifer demanded. Asmodeus stared, caught between pride and terror. He knew he was posturing, and worse, he knew Lucifer was aware of it. Lucifer shifted his attention to the questionable loyalists. "Ghom of the third circle, Chorozon of the sixth, and Formida of the House of Shadows, you initially rebelled against your lord, but according to my most loyal of kin, your minds were quickly changed when reminded of your loyalties. I'm more than sure the mighty Samgina left a great deal out regarding your alliance, but I've learned not to question him. It is his prerogative to share what he finds appropriate. Through his unwavering loyalty to the throne and Hell itself has he earned such liberties. You, my wayward kings, returned to the fold when you were needed, and for that, you will remain kings in your respective realms," Lucifer proclaimed. "And you, mighty Samgina, how may Hell show you its gratitude for being its champion?" Lucifer asked.

Samgina bowed. "My lord, the opportunity to fulfill my duty is more than thanks enough," Samgina responded graciously.

Lucifer chuckled, a sound rarely heard in Hell. "What kind of master would I be letting my champion walk away unrewarded for such a heroic deed?" Lucifer postured rhetorically. "Let it be known as of this moment in eternity that Samgina of the House of Sameal shall bear the title of king/ prince and champion of hell second in line to the throne"! Lucifer declared, his voice ringing in every fissure, cave, nook and cranny of Hell. Lucifer looked at a somewhat perturbed Samgina.

"My lord, I don't want . . ." Samgina trailed off as Lucifer raised his hand for silence.

"My brother, the only reason the rebels got as far as they did was because there was no clear line of succession. Now that problem has been solved, and I assure you, any enemy would prefer to fight me opposed to you. You still miraculously carry Heaven's light in you, and the demons are terrified of you, so if you would please accept the position as a favor to me. Besides, if my dark half tries to possess me, I need your power to stand up to me," Lucifer concluded.

Samgina bowed. "Under that very narrow condition, I accept," he stated seriously.

Lucifer bowed to Samgina. "Your Highness," Lucifer said, bowing seriously.

Samgina bowed in return. "Your Majesty," Samgina responded.

"Your Highness, the last one here was the heart of this rebellion and your usurpation from office. His judgment is in your hands," Lucifer concluded by waving his hand, and Samgina was transported to a throne room. In the middle of the huge chamber, curled, was the great dragon Elan.

"I like this chamber," he boomed.

Samgina nodded in agreement. "Yes, it seems nice enough," he admitted. Slowly he walked the expanse of the room, looking at the decor. His eyes locked on a familiar painting of the expulsion from Heaven when he and Lucifer was placed on the transformed body of Perdition and was cast out as a bolt of lightning, piercing the cosmos to create this which they called Hell. A note was attached. "With lowest regards, Lucifer." Samgina frowned deeply, knowing how much Lucifer favored that painting. Turning, he saw a glitter beyond Elan. He walk toward past the mighty dragon, who obstructed his view.

Elan's voice filled the chamber. "Look, they were considerate enough to not only give me space to rest comfortably, but look at that balcony! A launching perch if ever I've seen one, and the view!" Elan boomed.

As Samgina walked around Elan, he noticed the glitter was a reflection of a diamond throne with Elan's figure chiseled into it, but what was more enticing was what was or, rather, who was kneeling at the foot of his throne. Asmodeus. The King of Lust looked up and tried to rise to his feet, but the chains seemed to hold him to the floor.

CHAPTER

16

Samgina approached the struggling figure from the rear. Hearing his approach, Asmodeus ceased struggling. "Have you come to gloat, fallen one?" Asmodeus spat.

Samgina slowly walked past Asmodeus, staring at him. "You never knew me if that's what you think," Samgina responded.

"You have condemned Hell by siding with a weak leader," Asmodeus accused.

Samgina slowly ascended the dais to his throne. Slowly caressing the etching of Elan engraved masterfully on it, Samgina continued. "Such a shame you do not see the errors of your ways, slave," Samgina whispered with a force that rocked Asmodeus as his first judgment was pronounced and his mantle of kingship was stripped from him.

Now attired in the tattered robes of a slave and his power removed, the shriveled shadow of the would-be ruler of Hell stared at Samgina with fury in his alabaster eyes. "I know you have never thought more of me than a weak, lust-filled demon, but I'm more than that! I had ambitions, and your master sought to keep me confined in that damned circle so my goals would not see fruition!" Asmodeus complained.

Samgina frowned. "Oh, you think this is where you plead your case? That you might strike a chord that would somehow minimize your sentence?" Samgina asked.

Asmodeus, still defiant, feebly shrugged. "Do as you will to me, fallen. There is no judgment that can change my beliefs," Asmodeus growled.

Samgina frowned. "As you wish."

A cloud of smoke swirled, and Ghom, King of Gluttony, stepped through. He immediately bowed to the second in command of Hell. "My lord, how may I be of service?"

Samgina frowned. "First, by promising never to do that again." He greeted his royal brother.

"If you would like, I will refrain from doing it in private settings, but like it or not, Lucifer has named you successor, so it is customary to address you as such," Ghom clarified.

Samgina shrugged. "I guess that must suffice," he said, sounding dejected.

"How may I be of service, my lord?" Ghom inquired.

"Ah yes, the issue at hand. Well, seeing as how Asmodeus here had seen fit to cause you the most trouble, part, in fact, because of the proximity of your borders but also because of the massive influence you possess as the king of gluttony, I believe that it's appropriate to give to you as a gift a new slave," Samgina said, indicating the kneeling Asmodeus.

Ghom considered for a moment and frowned. "Come to think about it, yes, my lord, I can think of the perfect position for the former king of lust."

Samgina frowned deeply. "Do share," he said, curious as to what the King of Gluttony had in mind.

"It would seem that many of our picahs, minions, and slaves had their lustful desires quenched when the king here took to his rebellion and failed to foster the damning vices that kept our demonic brothers chained to Hell."

Samgina looked wondering. "And?" Samgina asked.

Ghom frowned widely. "It will awaken threefold when we reestablish the office."

"Let us do so," Samgina insisted.

"We call forth Minos, Judge of Hell," Ghom uttered.

Minos appeared, pointing at Asmodeus, who appeared to have finally understood his judgment had come. "You have been found guilty of sedition and treason. You have been judged!" Minos declared with damning finality. "We call forth from the pits of anguish Paris of Troy to step forth and be excelled as the new king of lust."

Paris of the ancient kingdom of Troy strode from the flames, his visage growing with power. He looked to Ghom and Samgina and bowed. "Your will be done," he cursed. Asmodeus shrunk to the size and took the shape of a tiny piglet. Samgina looked slightly confounded.

Ghom immediately clarified. "He is endowed with the curse of insatiability. He shall be offered as a source of sexual release to our male lower classes, forever begging to be raped with a portion of his mind fully aware and disgusted by the treatment he so voraciously begs for," Ghom shared, feeling pleased by the new successor of Hell's decision to hand over the traitorous piece of demon shit over to him. "Will that be all, my lord?" Ghom asked.

Samgina nodded affirmatively. "Yes, King Ghom, and we extend our thanks for your decision to join us in this battle."

Ghom frowned. "My lord, if I had not been so taken by the deceiver and the lustful, one doubt would have never come between us," Ghom admitted, abashed.

"What is done is done. When it mattered, you chose wisely by remembering your oath to Lucifer," Samgina stated. Ghom bowed and vanished. Samgina looked to his dragon. "What say you to a trip to the Dark Palace?" he inquired.

"You do realize as a king of Hell you may transport as you wish," Elan pointed out.

Samgina frowned. "I've always had that power, my brother. You are my preferred method of travel," Samgina stated.

The dragon roared and propped himself up. "Let us go," he roared. The denizens of the new midcircle (between reception and the second circle as laid out in Bischoff's design) looked up when they heard the roar of Elan and watched as their master and his brother flew into the depths of Hell.

Eternity

Lucifer gazed into eternity, feeling a familiar tug. After a timeless moment of watching universes being born and dying, he became aware of a familiar presence.

"Metatron," Lucifer said by way of greeting.

The majestic angel greeted him in turn, "Lucifer."

Lucifer looked at the one dubbed the Voice of God. Raising his hand and squinting because of Metatron's radiance, Lucifer cracked wise, "Want to turn down the lights there, twinkle?"

Metatron chuckled. "Forgive me. Sometimes I forget."

Lucifer shrugged, not believing him for a second. "We all have our cross to bear."

Metatron nodded in agreement. "I hope yours was not unbearable," Metatron said, sounding sincere.

Lucifer straightened his back. "We are Hell, sir. It is what we do. We bear the negative destructive forces of the universe and transpose it to a more harmonious state," he claimed with pride.

"That you do," Metatron agreed. "What now?" he inquired.

Lucifer looked at him, smirking. "Please let us not obfuscate. You know much more of the divine plan than I," Lucifer stated matter-of-factly.

"Indeed," admitted Metatron. "I just meant from your end of things," Metatron said, clarifying.

"Why are you here? The boss too busy to come and ask?" Lucifer teased.

Metatron nodded. "You've been busy, but the world took the baton and ran headfirst into dire events. There is plague, famine, war, and violence." Metatron stopped, interrupted by Lucifer.

"There have always been this things," Lucifer pointed out.

Metatron agreed. "But not at this scale. People are dying by the millions. Your gates shall soon know their fill," Metatron warned.

Lucifer frowned then smiled, remembering to whom he was speaking. "We got that covered. The renovation is moving along just fine," Lucifer reported.

Metatron smiled. "You're welcome," he said with a tinge of sarcasm.

Lucifer looked at Metatron sideways. "Okay, innuendo aside, you're not seriously going to stand here and try to take credit for the outcome of this fiasco?" he exclaimed.

Metatron's gaze looked out into eternity as if it were a cosmic ocean. "One of the few places where violence seems serene," he pointed out.

"Speaking of which," Lucifer interjected, "the level of violence in the mortal realm must be at all-time high if the Chairman needed Hell expanded, and if that's the case, the suffering must be extraordinary! How does this serve his purpose, and how does the Chairman justify or reward their suffering?" Lucifer asked curiously.

Metatron smiled and pointed to a spot in space. "See that region of the cosmos?" Metatron asked.

Lucifer followed to where the finger pointed. Staring for a moment, he quipped, "All I see is empty space."

Metatron's smile deepened. "Because emotions or the frequency equivalent of it cannot be seen except through the expression of the recipient," Metatron explained.

Lucifer looked at him, frustrated. "I know you think you explained yourself, but you didn't," Lucifer complained.

Metatron feigned surprise. "No?" he asked disingenuously.

Lucifer shook his head. "Not at all," he responded simply.

Metatron sighed. "Fine. For all those that came on the short bus—"

Lucifer interjected sharply. "Hey! You don't have to be an ass about it."

Metatron looked out of the corner of his eye at Lucifer. "As I was saying," Metatron continued, "all the suffering, pain, sorrow, and equivalent sonic frequencies are being stored in that region of space so that when mankind arrive in Heaven, that region's frequencies will be transmuted to joy and showered upon the souls when entering paradise," Metatron said with awe in his voice. He pretended not to see Lucifer wipe a tear from his eye.

"Okay," Lucifer snorted, "that is beautiful, almost poetic."

Metatron looked upon the Lord of Evil. "The Chairman is very proud of the effort you've put forth and congratulates you on the handling of your difficulties in Hell during these trying times," Metatron shared. Lucifer frowned. Metatron smiled. "Wrong zip code," he said offhandedly, making Lucifer smile.

The Dark Palace

Ibliss was at his desk when he received a summons. Entering the elaborate throne room, he made his way quickly to Lucifer, who sat on his throne. "My lord, how may I serve you?"

Lucifer looked at his diminutive assistant. What most didn't realize was that small-statured demon had vast powers, powers that rivaled most of the princes of Hell. "Ibliss, I would like my itinerary to begin with the master builder."

Ibliss scribbled. "And then, my lord?" he asked obediently.

"We'll play it by ear after that."

Ibliss shut his stylus. "As you command, my lord."

The master builder Karl Bischoff was the accredited designer of the Nazi death camps, which ushered millions into the cold embrace of death, who recently outbid the original designer Mulciber with a simple yet more efficient superimposed square or box pattern. This simple design eliminated the possibility of demonic or a damned soul escaping. The logic was insightful as Bischoff recognized that lesser demons, those involved with the actual application of punitive administration, were easily baffled when taxed (e.g., in the former conical shape, because of its circular formation, escapees could confuse the demon by doubling back and retracing his steps, circling the pursuing demon and approaching it from the rear). This method was referred to as demon humping by damned souls and was discovered by Bischoff during his term as a damned soul. Using this insight, Bischoff explained to Lucifer why the square was efficient. "As the Middle Easterners would say, 'It is so the devil may corner you.'" Lucifer had frowned at that, which gave a sense of value to the diabolical mass murderer.

Bischoff entered the throne room of the master of Hell. "My lord," Bischoff said while kneeling.

"Master Builder," Lucifer began, "how does one test the integrity of their work?" Lucifer inquired, leaving Bischoff on edge, because an open-ended question by a demon was an invitation to temptation. An invitation by the Lord of Demons was one to damnation. Bischoff chose his next words carefully.

"Well, my lord, first, there is cost of time, labor, and resources; second, the installation or proper allocation of said resources; and third, a concise, cohesive, and proper methodology of attaining desired goal," Bischoff finished, feeling satisfied with his answer.

Lucifer frowned at him. "You feel good about your answer, do you?" Lucifer asked. Bischoff felt the hairs on his neck stand. "Let's see," Lucifer quipped. "First, you took it upon yourself to take advantage of the situation by approaching the royalty of Hell and spoke to them as equals." Bischoff tried to interject, which was met by Lucifer's uplifted hand. "If you please," he stated, sounding irritated at the intended interruption. "Second," Lucifer continued, "you assumed to take liberties during the rebellion that allowed you to collect tithes and oaths of loyalties not due you." Bischoff opened his mouth only to find it sealed shut, as if never born with one. Horrified, he stared at Lucifer, who was staring back at him. "Do I have your attention now?" the Lord of Evil asked sarcastically. "Master Builder, you have acceded your authority and abused your position by assigning positions of power. Therefore, you shall be punished by the final means which you did not state in your confirmation of a completed project," Lucifer stated mildly.

Bischoff's eyes widened in terror as realization dawned upon him. His screams of anguish could be heard throughout Hell. It brought a frown to some demonic lips. Goebbels, who had retained his position, shook his head as he remembered his former colleague's glaring weakness. *The leader does not love you, Herr Bischoff.* He scoffed.

From: The Desk of Lucifer, King and Master of Hell, a.k.a. the Supervisor
To: The Lord Creator, a.k.a. Supreme Being, a.k.a. the Chairman

Boss,

As directed, Hell has been renovated to your specifications (bigger than shit). However, it has come at a steep price as many of my former employees have been found unsuitable or inflexible to the new order of things. That being said, new positions have been filled. Midas, ancient king of the Greeks, has been elevated from regent to king of the greed (fourth circle), displacing Mammon. Ghom has retained his kingdom and is officially King of Gluttony (third circle). Nazarick of the fifth circle (wrath) has been displaced, and the demon Azazel has been elevated as its king. Glabrezu, regent of the ninth circle (treachery), has been displaced and punished for his disobedience. The rebel kings, as well as Satan (my shadow of fury), has been placed on the newly formed ninth terrace, where their screams of punishment is bordered by the newly constructed Wall of Silence, which reflects their screams back upon them and spare its neighbor, that is, the House of Treachery. Formida of the House of Shadows has been elevated to be king of that circle. The hellhound Cerebus roams the renamed Avenue of the Damned as well as sitting beside Ghom as executioner of Ghom's will. The designer Karl Bischoff has been assigned to the inspection of each of his designs to assure their quality. In the hopes that this fulfills your demands upon your servants of Hell, I am Lucifer Morning Star, presiding supervisor of Hell.

Rex Perdition Infinitum.

Lightning Source UK Ltd.
Milton Keynes UK
UKHW041827270421
382745UK00007B/444/J